WHAT PEOPLE ARE SAYING ABOUT

Don't Doubt the Magic!

When I first interviewed Cathie Devitt I was intrigued by the story line of her first book *Don't Drink and Fly*, her characters feel so real that you know you know them from somewhere. Add a little magic gone wrong, a dash of some lies and whole lot of confusion and now you have a story that you want to read to the end.

With this second book *Don't Doubt the Magic!*, we see lies desperately trying to be covered up and a need to know the truth at all cost. Cathie has done it again and once more we are drawn into the mystery of the past and a desire to know what the future holds for the character Bernice, who has now turned to the Tarot to find her truth.

I love Cathie's story of why she became an author and being true to her own passion, so much so I will be interviewing her for the 3rd time very soon.

Sara Troy, www.selfdiscoveryradio.com

Cathie Devitt deftly brings two of Scotland's distinct and traditional cultures together; the claustrophobia of tight knit island life and the alienation of urban life. The characters are so sharply defined they feel like your own friends and relatives and she hasn't sugar coated the Gaelic culture either, choosing to present it in all its glorious darkness.

Imagine a Dan Brown novel but with the plot twists and turns being absolutely believable.

What a brilliant TV series this trilogy would make.

Des Dillon, www.desdillon.com

Don't Doubt the Magic!

The Story of Bernice O'Hanlon – Part Two

Don't Doubt the Magic!

The Story of Bernice O'Hanlon – Part Two

Cathie Devitt

Winchester, UK
Washington, USA

First published by Roundfire Books, 2017
Roundfire Books is an imprint of John Hunt Publishing Ltd., Laurel House, Station Approach,
Alresford, Hants, SO24 9JH, UK
office1@jhpbooks.net
www.johnhuntpublishing.com
www.roundfire-books.com

For distributor details and how to order please visit the 'Ordering' section on our website.

Text copyright: Cathie Devitt 2016

ISBN: 978 1 78535 601 8
978 1 78535 602 5 (ebook)
Library of Congress Control Number: 2016952464

A CIP catalogue record for this book is available from the British Library.

Design: Stuart Davies

Printed and bound by CPI Group (UK) Ltd, Croydon, CR0 4YY, UK

We operate a distinctive and ethical publishing philosophy in all
areas of our business, from our global network of authors to
production and worldwide distribution.

CONTENTS

This book is dedicated to: My beautiful, talented nieces:
Kathryn Devitt, Anna Devitt, Melissa Jarvis and Olivia Jarvis.
I am so proud to have watched you grow from babies into
intelligent young women.
Take charge of your lives and make every second count.
Love you.

Other Titles by Cathie Devitt

The story of Bernice O'Hanlon Part One:
"Don't Drink and Fly!":ISBN-13: 978-1782790167, 1782790160.

"This is the first novella of a trilogy, so even when we reach the end of the first stage of Bernice's journey, we know there'll be more drama waiting to unfold, and this reader, for one, is looking forward to enjoying more of the potent new voice on Scotland's literary scene that is Cathie Devitt."
Brian Whittingham – poet, playwright, editor, and teacher of Creative Writing in Glasgow. He has also taught at Seattle University as a visiting professor.

"Don't Drink & Fly!" centring on a free spirited Wiccan witch, Bernice O'Hanlon, deftly brings two of Scotland's distinct and traditional cultures together; the claustrophobia of tight knit island life and the alienation of urban life. The characters are so sharply defined they feel like your own friends and relatives and Cathie Devitt hasn't sugar coated the Gaelic culture either, choosing to present it in all its glorious darkness."
Des Dillon, internationally acclaimed award-winning writer, broadcaster, playwright and teacher of Creative Writing.

"Moving between an unpolished Glasgow and a complex island community, Devitt's magical mayhem conceals shadowy family secrets. Bernice and Maggie, amidst spells and betrayals uncover a multitude of duplicities which tests and ultimately cements the bonds of their friendship. Sad and funny in equal measure Cathie Devitt's "Don't Drink And Fly" is the first of what I hope will be many adventures for Bernice, the Wiccan witch."
Laura Marney, is a novelist and teaches the MLitt Creative Writing programme at Glasgow University.

"Don't Drink & Fly!" Is a story of struggles, dark family secrets, and people haunted by the past. It is a confusing, messy sort of setup which is a good deal more like life than fiction, and as a consequence makes a nice change in a novel. I could not work out where it was going, and it kept surprising me. This is something I like in a story, rather than neatly explained, everything clear and reasonably predictable writing. The Paganism in this story is recognisable to me, this is the kind of witchcraft that fits into my world, these are characters I could imagine meeting down the pub. It's grounded and fantastical in equal measure, and I really like how the magical elements are handled".
Nimue Brown Writer.

Preface

This is Part Two of my trilogy of novellas about the life of fictional character, Bernice O'Hanlon. Each of the three parts can easily be devoured on their own. Think of them as literary tapas. I hope you are hungry!

I created the character of Bernice after I discovered the world of Wicca. I love to explore different cultures and living in an area that has a history of the persecution of witches, I was keen to find out just what the term "witch" means in today's modern world. Part of my research was speaking to a range of people who practice Wicca, also reading books by professionals in the field such as; Raymond Buckley and Gerald Gardiner, taking part in Sabbat celebrations and other events such as the annual International Festival "Witchfest", held previously in London and organised by "The Children of Artemis". There are proposals to re-locate to Brighton. (See Doreen Valiente Museum, Brighton).

I have created a network of people who are happy for me to discuss the path they have chosen and why. We talk about how Wicca fits into their lives and the reaction of others when they tell them that they are a witch. I found that many of my own beliefs and practices were similar to those practiced in the Wiccan community. I have for a long time enjoyed the benefits of natural herbs and remedies, which are part of Wiccan culture. I have a collection of crystals because I love the look and feel of them. I am now more educated in their properties, use and benefits. There are many aspects of Wicca which seem to me to be common sense and all about being a decent human being who respects others and appreciates the wonders of nature.

The story of Bernice is one of intrigue and mystery, with a dash of humour, and explores the delicate intricacies of relationships.

Many readers who enjoyed "Don't Drink & Fly!" contacted me for more information about Wicca. With this in mind I have include some explanations and a glossary of terminology.

Acknowledgements

Thank You...

My writer's bloke Brian, for his patience, understanding, and constructive criticism.

Mandy Sinclair www.mandysinclair.com for her artistic input for cover ideas.

John Hunt Publishing www.johnhuntpublishing.com for the time and support of your editorial and production staff.

Children of Artemis www.witchcraft.org for welcoming me to facilitate a workshop at Witchfest International.

Pauline Reid www.bewitchingbeauty.co.uk for letting me into your Pagan world, circle of friends and fantastic home which is a shrine to the craft.

Sara Troy www.selfdiscoveryradio.com for her amazing positivity and support.

Arvon Foundation – The Hurst – www.arvon.org for giving me the time and space at their retreat to edit this book.

Introduction

For Bernice, going back to the island where she was raised by her grandparents was a difficult but necessary journey. On the news of her granny's death, Bernice found new strength to confront the man she saw as being the primary cause of her estrangement from the woman who raised her and introduced her to the spiritual world that she embraced.

The confrontations that follow with others raise more questions and revelations than anyone should have to deal with, but deal with them she must.

There was a crowd back at the farm speculating about her fractured life. The noise was unbearable. Though the gathering was her idea, Bernice felt the need to escape.

Drawn to the beach, despite the darkness and chill in the air, she knew that the waters would soothe her.

Chapter 1

Nick grabbed at his chest as he ran the last few yards towards the shore calling her name. 'Bernice! Be-r-nice!' His calls went unanswered.

'It's not a good time for skinny dipping in Scotland,' he mumbled as he glanced from left to right and left again before spotting her in the water. Scrunching the fabric of his shirt tighter he sprinted towards her.

Bernice turned at the sound of his voice. She rose with the sea at waist level and began walking towards him with slow, deliberate strides.

'Bernice!' Nick stumbled, falling to his knees with the effort of his mad dash. She flopped down beside him, her hair tumbling like seaweed across her face.

'Sleep jogging?' She laughed.

Nick pulled at his tie and spluttered. 'Looking,' he coughed, 'for you.'

She pressed a finger to his lips and pulled his head onto her lap. Pushing her hair behind her ears, she let the heavy mane drip down her back.

'For me, you came looking for me?'

Nick cleared his throat and nodded.

'How did you know I was here?'

'Bernice! I thought you were at the last stop before the terminus.'

'Eh, you've got it all wrong, Nick. I wanted away from the bedlam, that's all. I needed a bit of space.'

'Bedlam? They're all there for *you*. You asked them to be.'

'So? Now I want to be here.' Bernice pulled an atheme from her bag and began to draw a circle on the sand. 'Sit with me, Nick.'

Nick shuffled closer. He blew on his hands. 'You must be

freezing.' He slipped off his jacket and draped it around her shoulders. Bernice continued to carve the circle.

'What's with the knife?'

'Atheme, Nick.' She paused. 'A-tha-may.'

'What are you like with your weird language?'

'It's Wiccan not weird.'

Nick watched closely as Bernice placed four candles on the sand. She trod softly around the circle, setting a candle at each of the four quarters. 'North, South, East, West.'

Nick admired the colours as she lit each one. 'Traffic Lights?' he asked.

'Green for earth, red for fire, yellow for air and blue for water,' Bernice explained.

'Bernice? Don't you think we should be getting back to your guests?'

'I have guests?' Her throaty laugh was almost melodic. 'I want to connect with the deities not the dafties. Will you join me?'

'No. I'll sit here and make sure you don't get arrested or measured for a nice white coat with lots of buckles.'

'It's your loss. You know, the universe has a pretty good sense of humour and we mortals are fallible. You need to open up to new ideas, embrace challenge.'

Nick lay back on the sand and stared at the dark sky, barely aware of Bernice as she moved within the circle, her voice soft and low. He closed his eyes and thought back over the previous few weeks. No wonder Bernice was losing control. Nick could see why she might want to end it all, but no, she leaves her own granny's wake to prance about the beach in a circle of candles.

Bernice poked him in the side with her toe. 'Come on Rumpelstiltskin, suppose we should head back. I'm done here for now.'

Nick helped Bernice pack away her tools. Her hand brushed his and he looked into her eyes a bit longer than he probably should have.

'I know it's been difficult and exhausting but those folk back at the farm are on your side.'

'You think?' Bernice asked.

He let his gaze drop, confused by the effect that Bernice was having on him. 'Okay. I've a bar to run. We need to make plans to get back to Glasgow. Life goes on.'

'Life goes on for some,' Bernice whispered. 'This island is where my life began.'

Nick sighed. 'Look, this has all been very stressful. I get that. But surely you feel better knowing that you still have family. Liam?'

'I don't believe that nonsense about Liam. He can't be my brother, and I can feel he's not my son.'

'It was 20 years ago, Bernice. You were young and afraid, your head wasn't in the right place. Dermott wouldn't lie. Why would he? If he says Liam is your brother, just accept that. Your son, Humiel, you need to let the past go. You lost him, Bernice. Hanging onto false hope is driving you crazy.'

'I'm not saying Dermott's lied knowingly, but Granddad worked him and Robbie like puppets. They're not the sharpest lemons in the gin. Think about it. If Liam is Granny's son, he's my uncle, not my brother. They say he's my brother?'

Nick scratched his head. 'Unless? Unless McShane and your granny had a relationship?'

'This isn't a Hollywood film script. This is my life. Someone is lying. It just doesn't add up. None of it does.'

Look, we really need to get back. That note you left at the farm tonight? A bit cryptic don't you think? Or was that your plan? Looking for attention? You made it pretty difficult for Maggie and Stacey. We thought you were off to top yourself.'

'Like mother like daughter?'

'Your mother's death was an accident.'

'Was it? You know, until tonight, I was terrified of the sea. Those waves can drag you down. All that space below. Ever

3

heard of the term "Ordeal by water," Nick?'

'Something about witches being thrown into water to prove they were in cahoots with the devil?'

'That's about right. Suspected of being a witch you were thrown into deep water. If you drowned you were innocent, floating meant you were guilty, and sentenced to death, probably by fire. Bit of a raw deal, eh? '

'We're in a different century, Bernice. Things have moved on.'

'No they haven't. Society just made up new words for persecution: apartheid/homophobia/anti-semitism/sectarianism /racism, and don't start me on bullying. Do you realise how many folk suffer in silence because schoolmates, workmates, even family and friends tease them to the point that they just can't face another day?'

'Oh, Bernice, please, it's not the same.'

They walked back to the car park without speaking, a bedraggled couple with an invisible, widening gap between them.

Neither noticed the car that followed a few lengths behind as they pulled out of the parking bay.

Chapter 2

Back at the farmhouse, the wake was well and truly over. Granny had been mourned and praised and most of the buffet was gone. Maggie was busy clearing away the debris. Stacey and Liam lay snuggled under a duvet on the sofa.

'Honey, I'm Home!' Bernice called out as she came through the front door. 'Just off for a quick shower.' She took the stairs two at a time, leaving Nick to find Maggie in the kitchen.

'Is that it? She's just going upstairs? She gives no explanation, nothing?' Maggie wiped down a worktop.

'Have you been crying, Maggie?' He touched her shoulder and she pulled away.

Stacey hobbled into the kitchen still draped in the duvet. She rubbed her eyes. 'Is Bernice okay?' she asked Nick.

'Of course she is.' Maggie poured dregs down the sink. 'Bernice is always okay. Goes off like a firecracker and leaves us to clear up the mess.'

'I said Liam and I would help in the morning, Mum.' Stacey pulled the duvet tighter.

Maggie banged a tumbler down so hard that it splintered. She gasped.

'You've cut yourself.' Nick grabbed Maggie's hand and pushed it under running water. They both watched her blood swirl like raspberry ripple down the plughole. Maggie pulled her hand away and grabbing a tea towel pressed down hard on the cut.

'This is all so crazy,' she sobbed. 'I want to go back to Glasgow. I don't want any more to do with this spooky island. It's full of psychopaths and half breeds.'

Liam stood beside Stacey. 'You're mum isn't talking about the mess from the party, Stacey. Are you?'

Maggie sucked her bleeding finger and turned away.

'Why don't you and Liam head upstairs? Things always look better after a night's sleep.' Nick scooped coffee granules into two mugs.

Maggie wiped her nose and leaned against the sink.

'Come on, let's go through and have a cuppa. It's been a long night.' Nick led the way.

The ceilings in the farmhouse were low. The walls white-washed but stained with nicotine. An old hearth warmed the small room. Years before, the situation could have been quite romantic.

With the two youngsters out of the way, Maggie began to speak. 'How strange is all of this?'

Nick shook his head.

Maggie continued. 'It's like a nightmare, but real. I thought Bernice was coming to terms with it all. I thought she'd found closure.'

Nick glanced around the cramped room. He felt like he'd travelled back in time with the heavy furnishings and brassware. He noticed a small tapestry on a side wall and leaned closer to admire it. The delicate needlework made the image look three-dimensional: a cluster of bluebells, tied with the palest ribbon.

Bernice walked into the room. She wore a dark purple kaftan trimmed with gemstones and a towel wrapped around her head like a turban.

'This is cosy. You two want to be alone?' Bernice smiled.

'Grab a coffee, Bernice. We need to talk,' Nick suggested.

Bernice sat beside Nick. 'I'm tired. I'll skip the caffeine. What do you want to talk about?'

'You invite the village idiots and their cronies here and then go wandering off for a midnight swim. Have you any idea how that went?' Maggie snapped.

'No idea, tell me.'

'They already have you down as a screwball. This just added fuel...'

'To the fire?' Bernice glanced at Nick. 'They were getting a fire ready for me?'

Nick rested his hand on Maggie's knee. 'The fact is, we've all tried to support you through this, but Maggie's right, we need to get back to our own lives in Glasgow, with or without you, Bernice.'

Silence hung like cobwebs from the beamed ceiling. Bernice settled back on the sofa. 'You know how much it meant for me to come back to the island. I really thought I could find the answers but I'm no further forward. I need to know what happened to Humiel.'

'Humiel? You lost your son in childbirth. Just accept that. He's buried with your mother in the church cemetery.'

Maggie gasped. 'No. He isn't. I can feel him close to me at times. Grandad was a liar through and through, and as for McShane, he's so pickled in Poitin he'd sell his soul to the devil, although, I doubt if even he of the cloven hooves would want a soul as dark as McShane's in his collection.'

Nick pressed his finger to his lips. 'Shush.' He spoke slowly. 'Bernice. What happened to you was horrific. You don't want to bring charges against McShane and that's your call. The old guy's on his way out anyway. He has The Grimm Reaper stalking him. He's told you where Humiel is buried. Unless you want to go to court and get the grave exhumed, you need to accept what he says. Accept and move on. Look, I know you don't want your grandad buried anywhere near, but what about Granny? Why do you think Grandad wanted her cremated?'

'Because he had something to hide. You can't do an autopsy on a pile of ash.'

Maggie stood up sharply. 'So now you think your grandad murdered your granny? Are you serious? You couldn't make this up.'

Bernice turned to her friend. 'Has no one ever told you fact can be stranger than fiction?'

'The only fact here, Bernice is that you have lost the plot, totally lost it.' Maggie's face flushed as she clenched her fists by her side. 'I love you. I support you.' She paused.

'Now for the Abbott theory,' said Bernice, 'ah, but...'

Nick interrupted. 'You have to admit this is way too creepy to make sense.'

'I don't think Grandad murdered Granny. I never said that. Maybe it's you two who are jumping to conclusions.'

Maggie drank her coffee and stared into the mug.

'You're right. I don't want Grandad anywhere near my true family. But then I don't think the church cemetery is where they are. '

'So where are Granny and Humiel buried then?'

'Grandad did me a favour in a way. It would make him cringe, but really, until I find out the truth, better that I give Granny the send-off she would've wanted.'

'We've had the funeral service, Bernice, the reception afterwards and the crazy shindig last night. How many send-offs do you plan to have?'

Bernice plucked a pouch of Tarot cards from a shelf and began to spread them on a low table between herself and Maggie.

'You seem stressed. We all need a little guidance at times. Shuffle and choose six cards.'

'I don't need guidance. I need to get back to normality.' Maggie lowered her voice. 'Oh go on then if it shuts you up.'

Bernice watched closely as Maggie turned each card in sequence.

'Now let's see what we have. A quick look, humour me,' Bernice said. 'How you feel about yourself now, *The Hierophant*. What you most want at this moment, The *High Priestess*, Your fears, *The Tower*. What's going for you? *Judgement*. What's going against you. *The Star*. Last one, to show the outcome according to your current situation or the question you asked, *The Magician*. Are you sure you don't want me to explain the reading?'

'Just give me the bottom line,' Maggie replied.

'It won't take long to go over each card?' Bernice smiled.

Maggie knew very little about Tarot despite Bernice having explained the basics to her on various occasions. She bundled up the cards and handed them to Bernice. 'I don't understand any of this. Just tell us what you plan to do about your granny's ashes.'

Bernice rubbed the cards with sea salt and tucked them back into the velvet pouch she had taken them from.

'I'm taking Granny's ashes to a memorial forest, way over on the north side of the island.

'Of course you are.' Nick stood, stretched and yawned. 'Sorry, but I'm struggling to keep my eyes open.'

'I'm shattered too,' Maggie agreed.' We'll talk in the morning.

They left Bernice sketching funeral urns on a pad in the glow of the log fire.

Chapter 3

Mrs McEwan sat on a deck chair outside the post office: not a usual sight in the village on such a cold morning. On the pavement beside her lay a bale of newspapers. She plucked one at a time from the pile, scribbled on the top right corner, folded the paper in three and stuffed it into a canvas satchel, stopping only to blow on the fingerless gloves she was wearing.

'What you doing out here?' The postman asked, arriving at his usual time.

Mrs McEwan bent her head towards the door. 'He's tarting up the shop, I can't stand fumes.'

'Away with you, woman, paint don't have fumes nowadays, get yourself inside.' He brushed past her.

Mrs McEwan continued with her task. 'Fiddly this is,' she murmured.

A voice called from inside the shop. 'Tea's ready! No licence for a pavement café, so you'll need to come through.' Mr McEwan and the postman were already engaged in conversation when Mrs McEwan toddled towards them. She had the satchel slung across her back and was nudging the stack of newspapers slowly across the floor with her foot.

'Sit down, woman,' Mr McEwan said.' You'll be doing yourself an injury.' He steered her towards a chair and handed her a cup and saucer.

'So what's this really about?' The postman asked.

'Oh, she's scared she'll miss something. Parking herself outside to make sure she doesn't.

'Am I missing something?' The postman asked.

'It's all that carry on up at O'Hanlon's farm, with their Bernadette still hanging around trying to stir up trouble. Sure, did you not hear about her shenanigans the night of the funeral?' Mr McEwan asked.

'Which funeral would that be? It seems like they've a standing order with the hearse lately.'

'Oh, she never went to her grandad's, just gave strict instructions he was to be buried outside of the church grounds. Dermott took charge of all that. No, she only goes and throws a party to say her goodbyes to her 'aul granny on the very night the old man was laid to rest. Open invitation. Of course, we only went out of curiosity.' Mrs McEwan bubbled over with excitement.

Mr McEwan grunted.

'Disrespectful you think? You've no idea about that man – blood of ice and a heart of stone.' Mrs McEwan's interest was re-ignited. 'I've tried talking to her, but Bernadette O'Hanlon is not one to open up easily.

'Should my ears be burning?' Bernice smiled as she entered the shop.

'Not at all love, sure I'm on your side. Good friend of your granny, you know.' Mrs McEwan bustled behind the counter. 'What can I get for you?'

The two men turned away.

'Nice colour.' Bernice tapped an open paint tin. 'Puce is it?'

'None of that fancy pants stuff. It's magnolia. You can't go wrong with magnolia.'

'No, don't suppose you can. You class yourself as a good friend of Granny's do you?'

'Of course, Bernadette, anything you want to know, you only have to ask.'

'Bernice. Please. Bernadette is long gone. I'll have two bread rolls and a copy of the rag.' She pointed at the newspapers. 'Are you still taking adverts for the window?'

'One fifty a week or a fiver a month. Are you clearing the house?'

'No. I want to place this.' Bernice handed over a postcard.

Mrs McEwan shook her head. 'I'm not sure this is the kind of thing we want to have in the window. Maybe The Courier would be better?'

Bernice paid for her goods and tucked the postcard inside the newspaper. 'You could be right. I'll give them a bell.' She turned to walk away and paused. 'For the record, Granny never regarded you as a friend, an acquaintance perhaps, but never quite a friend.'

'I know more about your life than you want to hear,' the older woman replied.

'Really, you know or you have a patched up Chinese whisper version to tell me?'

'Well, if that's your attitude, go ahead – search away, but without my help you'll struggle to make any sense of it.'

Bernice rested her elbows on the counter. 'Go on then, tell me. Once upon a time...?'

Mr McEwan returned and lifted the pot of paint. He tipped his cap in Bernice's direction. Mrs McEwan busied herself with sorting the counter and tutted loudly.

'We'll continue this some other time then?' Bernice smiled and left.

Mr McEwan dipped a brush into the paint.

'Get a roller or you'll be painting all month!' his wife snapped. 'I've a headache. I'm going for a lie down.

Mr McEwan sighed, turned up his radio and singing along to the local channel he carried on smothering the walls in paint the colour of curdled milk.

* * *

'The cheek of her,' Mrs McEwan mumbled as she pulled an old vanity case from the top of her wardrobe. It wasn't locked. 'Swans off to the city for years then glides back like little Miss Innocent, I'll show her.' The case was pale-pink, hand-stitched, with a faded image of ballet pumps on one side. Beside the lock, a small monogram was barely readable. As she lifted the lid to reveal a bundle of letters, she disturbed a layer of dust and sneezed.

'Thinks she's so clever, eh?' Mrs McEwan stroked the envelopes as though reassuring herself that she held the upper hand. 'Oh, she'll come to me in time.'

Mrs McEwan looked out of her bedroom window. Bernice was chatting to a man. He was short, sturdy and wore dirty work clothes. Mrs McEwan strained to focus.

Bernice motioned with her hands. Mrs McEwan was too far away to capture the look on her face. The man scratched under his cap and shifted from foot to foot.

Bernice grabbed his sleeve at one point and moved her face closer to his. The man nodded and shrugged.

Mrs McEwan watched as the figure walked away. His gait was familiar. He stopped and unbridled an old Clydesdale mare from a fence.

"Now I wonder what would Bernadette want with the black-smith?" Mrs McEwan's brow creased.

Chapter 4

Maggie was quiet on the ferry back to the mainland. Despite the sharp wind, she chose to sit on the upper deck.

Nick tapped her arm with his elbow. 'Got you coffee and a cookie, nudge up.'

Maggie shifted along the damp bench and took the coffee.

'I knew Bernice had family troubles in her past. I'm not sure leaving her on the island's such a good idea. Not on her own.'

'You surprised?' Maggie asked. 'She's told me the story often enough.'

'More shocked than surprised. I thought she just ran away from home, and her granny? The way Bernice spoke about her I thought she was a hundred and three and there she was popping out kids into her forties. Who would have thought the boy, Liam, would turn up in my bar?'

'Bernice isn't convinced that Granny did have more children, not at her stage in life. Strange how Liam ends up in Glasgow though? Right before Bernice's granny dies.'

Nick lowered his head. 'You think Liam is Bernice's son, the baby she thought died at birth?'

'She seems convinced that he's not.'

'Liam called Granny, Ma.'

'So did Dermott and Robbie, but they weren't even family.'

'Here am I thinking I had it bad with my old dears but they are Boy Scouts compared to Bernice's mob. Don't think family is all it's cracked up to be.'

Maggie wiped an eyelash from her cheek. 'No, you're probably right.'

A seagull perched on the rail behind them and strutted along, dipping its head to check out if they had any crumbs to scavenge.

'Did you know that seagulls are very clever? They stamp their feet in a group to imitate rainfall and trick earthworms to come to the surface. Then they eat the wee slithers.' Nick laughed.

'No, but I did know that the seagull represents a carefree attitude, versatility and freedom.' Maggie broke a chunk of biscuit off. 'In Native American symbolism.'

'Is that not doves?'

'I think doves represent peace.' Maggie paused. 'I made a mistake marrying Wredd.'

Nick scuffed his boots along the deck.

'Don't you think I made a mistake, Nick?'

'Not for me to judge, never having made that scary trip down the aisle myself.'

'Do you think we'd still be together if you hadn't left when you did?'

'Don't know. Maybe you were right. We were very young.' Nick turned up the collar of his jacket.

'Older and wiser now though and life isn't looking any brighter.'

'You've got Stacey. Surely the marriage was worth that?'

Maggie held a biscuit out to the seagull. With precision, the bird swooped, caught the offering in its beak and flew away. Maggie gazed as it made a graceful ascent into the clouded sky.

'Ever wish you could do that? Just fly away to somewhere better. No baggage.'

Nick shrugged. 'Somewhere over the rainbow, Judy Garland style? Sure.'

'Speaking of birds, what are the lovebirds up to?'

'Oh, Liam and Stacey are wrapped around each other in the cabin. Feel sorry for Liam. Bernice isn't the only one hurting in all of this.'

Maggie stood to leave. 'It's getting cold now, maybe we should join them.'

Nick lifted the empty cups. A lid fell and blew along in front of him. Maggie was already on the stairs down to the cabin. A heavy boot trapped the lid. Nick bent to pick it up but the boot didn't move. He tugged it slightly and looked up. The man was not for shifting. His jacket had a hood that wasn't pulled up against the threatening downpour. A checked cap flopped over one eye, while a woollen scarf covered the lower half of his face.

'I've got it. Thanks.' Nick tugged again and the man raised his boot to release the lid. Nick tossed the rubbish into a swing bin and didn't look back. If he had, he would have seen the man move into a sheltered spot and speak into a small Dictaphone before lighting up a cigarette which he happily sucked on until the ferry docked at the mainland.

* * *

The ramp lowered and cars drove off. Heavy chains droned a rusty ballad as the gaggle of passengers disembarked. The man watched from the upper deck until he saw the foursome walk towards the pier. Maggie with her head bent against the rain. Nick striding beside her, with Stacey and Liam trailing closely behind, hand in hand, Stacey's laughter audible even from that distance.

The man felt a warm splash on what little of his face was visible. He drew his hand across the white deposit and cursed. 'Flying rats!' he bellowed as the seagull soared into the distance.

Chapter 5

Back on the island, Dermott looked through a window of the farmhouse. Bernice sat on an armchair by the fire, a glass with a crystal studded stem in her hand. Dermott tapped the window then moved towards the door. Bernice glanced over her shoulder but didn't rise. Dermott knocked and pushed it open.

'That'll be you in then,' Bernice said.

Dermott stood on the threshold. 'We never needed permission before.'

'Pull up a chair.' Bernice gestured towards the other armchair. Dermott sat down and stared at her.

'What?' Bernice asked.

'I'll get to the point.'

'Wish someone would.' Bernice laughed.

Dermott kept staring at her.' You can't just come back and take the farm.'

Bernice poured red wine into the glass. 'Why's that then?'

Dermott snorted. 'This is our home, mine and Robbie's. We've nowhere else to go.'

Bernice sipped the drink. It stained her lips.

'We've kept this place going over the years. Bed and board and little else we got for our efforts.'

'Were you held prisoner here?'

Dermott grunted. 'Of course not.'

'So why didn't you leave? Get your own place?'

'Oh, it was alright for you to drift off to the city. Make a new life. We never had that option.'

Bernice chewed the end of her hair and twisted it around her fingers like copper wire.

'I could've left I suppose, but Robbie? Well, he doesn't cope easily with change.'

'Your brother's a half-wit and you're the other half.'

Dermott reached for the bottle. 'I could do with a drink.'

Bernice snatched it back. 'Have a good gargle of Grandad's whiskey then. You know where it is.'

Dermott pulled open the door in a long wooden cabinet and returned with a stubby tumbler and half-empty bottle. The amber nectar glinted in the firelight. He downed a quick shot and poured another. 'Can we talk about this reasonably? What use is this place to you?'

'No use at all.'

So?' His eyes brightened.

'So? I'm not leaving here until I find out the truth about my family. Then…'

'Then?'

'Depends on how helpful folks are and what I find out. Been a long time coming, and I won't be rushed.'

Dermott leaned forwards.' Berna…Bernice. None of what happened was down to me or Robbie, so why are you punishing us? We're simple folk. We just want to lead a peaceful life.'

'Peace? Do you think I've found peace?'

Dermott took another shot of whiskey. 'Leave the past where it is. We can't change it.'

'No, we can't, but maybe, if I know the truth, I can understand the past. Until then I'm going nowhere.'

They heard footsteps on the path outside and the front door was again pushed open. Mrs McEwan stood in the doorway, she seemed quite breathless.

'We need to talk.' She pulled off her coat, sat on a dining chair and placed a large shopping bag on the table.

Bernice laughed. 'We need to talk? You all got the same script? I don't need to talk. I need to listen, to the truth. You lot wouldn't know the truth if it bit you on the bum.'

'No need for cursing, and in your grandparent's home too.' Mrs McEwan tapped her forehead, both shoulders and clasped her hands to her chest, then kissed a pendant around her neck in contrast. The chain held a gold pentagram.

'Here take the comfy seat.' Dermott stood.

'No, not at all, I'm fine where I am.'

'That's right. You stay near the door so you can make a quick getaway in case my cursing contaminates you,' Bernice slurred. She wiped her brow and set her glass on the table.

Dermott and Mrs McEwan watched as Bernice sank further into the chair. Her head flopped to one side and she started to snore.

'Drinking in the middle of the day is it?' Mrs McEwan cleared the table, washed the glass and poured what little of the wine was left down the sink. She patted her hands dry with a tea towel.

'This place needs a good scrub. What's she still doing here?'

'I've no idea. Just keeps saying she wants the truth.'

Mrs McEwan emptied some rubbish into a polythene bag and tied it in a knot. She handed the bag to Dermott.

'Put that outside. Come back and help me get her into bed. Maybe she'll sleep it off.' She lifted a tub of pills and read the label. 'Dr Manson must have prescribed these. I'm sure they shouldn't be washed down with alcohol. No wonder she's in such a state.'

'She will be alright won't she?' Dermott held the bin bag in his hand.

'Of course she will. Just do as I ask and stop whinging. I suppose I'll need to sort this out, same as I always do.'

Dermott banged the door behind him. Mrs McEwan slipped the pill bottle into her handbag. She lifted Bernice's eyelids one at a time and was checking her pulse when Dermott reappeared.

'What's wrong with her?'

'Drunk as a skunk that's all. Now let's get her shifted.'

* * *

With Bernice tucked up in bed, Dermott paced the floor. Mrs

McEwan rustled together a few sandwiches and a pot of tea. She set them on the table. 'Sit.' She poured the tea. 'Will you sit, Dermott?'

Dermott sat. He grabbed at the bread and stuffed it greedily into his mouth. 'Do you…?'

'Not with your mouth full. How much does Robbie know?'

Dermott shrugged and reached for another sandwich.

'Liam?'

Dermott chewed quickly, took a long swallow of tea and answered. 'Liam would have been fine if he'd stayed here. They've got him thinking all sorts in the city.'

Mrs McEwan clicked her tongue. 'It was always going to happen. Such a shame Granny passed afore that auld barstirt man of hers.'

Dermott finished off the snack. 'Is there any cake?'

Mrs McEwan tapped the back of his hand with a breadknife. 'Forget your belly for once would you?'

'My auld man says he's sorry. He was drunk. He says he doesn't mind much about that night – apart from her wearing a short skirt and silver shoes,' Dermott said.

'I do! I remember that night clear as angel tears. What a state that girl was in.'

'She couldn't get the law involved now though? He's an old man.'

'The thing that matters is, Bernice says she's not out for revenge, just wants to know what happened to the baby. What did she call him again?'

'Humiel. Never heard a name like it.'

'Tam McShane is looking for penance, forgiveness even. Let's just hope the cancer finishes him off before she can stir up any more dirt.' Mrs McEwan passed Dermott a napkin.

Dermott belched.' He is my father. I should feel sorry for him.'

'Do you?'

Dermott clenched his fists.

'Do you feel sorry for him?' Mrs McEwan asked again.

'I need to get back. Robbie's in a right state, he hates staying at Clancy's. He wanted to come with me. '

'Maybe you should have let him come. Soften her heart a bit? I can't see her keeping this place on. Sure, she must have her own place in Glasgow, work to get back to. Do you think that Nick's her fancy man?'

'Don't care. Just want her off the island.' Dermott twisted his hands together. 'I never knew. I never knew any of it.'

'Well, you know now. We'll get this sorted. Go see to Robbie. I'll douse the fire and let her sleep.'

Mrs McEwan lifted the tub of pills from her handbag and re-read the label. She recognised the brand name for Hormone Replacement Tablets.

"She must be going through an early menopause," thought Mrs McEwan, "that will be why she's so keen to find out about her son. I think Bernice has left it too late to have another child of her own. It makes sense now, her being so keen to revisit her past."

Chapter 6

Maggie was glad to be back in the city. She opened the windows of her home. 'Let some air in.'

Stacey shivered theatrically. 'I'm not going back to college.'

'I'd figured that. What are your plans then?' Maggie unpacked her holdall and started sorting washing into piles.

'Nick said I can work at the bar until I find something better.'

'Did he? Nice to know you went to him first.' Maggie sniffed a sock.

'Your dad's away and we have enough going on with Bernice.'

Maggie tossed the sock onto the "darks" pile.

'Mum?'

'That'll be me.'

'Has Dad left for good?'

Maggie slammed the door of the washing machine.

'Mum?'

The phone rang and Maggie went to answer it.

Stacey watched her mother nod, shrug, nod again, wind the flex around her wrist and finally hang up.

Maggie went back into the kitchen. She measured soap powder into a plastic beaker.

'You could see a counsellor? Lots of people have marriage problems.' Stacey stood with her hands on her hips. 'Mum?'

Maggie didn't reply.

'Who was calling, who were you speaking to?'

Maggie clicked the washing machine into action and it hummed softly.

'Who…was…that…on…the…phone?'

'Sales call,' Maggie lied.

'I'm thinking of moving in with Liam.'

Maggie let out a muffled laugh. 'You two plan to move into that pokey dive of a bedsit?'

'We're in love.'

'Of course you are and with both of you in bar work. You think you'll earn enough before love goes out the window. Don't talk daft. That flea pit doesn't even have its own bathroom.'

'I was thinking,' Stacey hesitated, 'if we paid you rent, we could live here?'

Maggie turned to her daughter.

'You hardly know him. He hardly knows himself. There's no way Liam's moving in here.'

Stacey grabbed her handbag. 'Dad would let him. Dad would want me to be happy. Dermott said Liam's Bernice's brother. Isn't that reference enough?' She rushed to the front door and called back. 'We don't need your validation!'

Maggie sat in her kitchen watching clothes tumble and tangle in the machine, finding the humming of the drum soothing until it reached a crescendo and whined into fast spin. She picked up a newspaper that Stacey had been scribbling on, "Flats to rent" circled in red ink. Maggie scrunched the paper and was about to throw it into the bin when a magazine slipped from the pages. An advert caught her attention. She spread the paper out on the worktop and smoothed the creases from a photo image.

It was him, her old boss, MacIntosh, opening yet another salon. So you're back then, she thought. "Local entrepreneur returns from business trip abroad with a wealth of ideas to bring the latest health and beauty experiences to the area", she read.

"I have the best products, the best equipment and the best systems. Now all I need are staff to compliment the business with their professional expertise." The advert went on to list a range of services and noted the details for recruitment. Maggie flipped over the pages of the glossy supplement and frowned.

The sound of the telephone broke her trail of thought. 'Hello?' Her shoulders dropped. 'No. I told you it wasn't a good time to talk.' She paused. 'What do you mean you saw Stacey leave?' Maggie pulled a curtain aside and looked out of her living room window. She looked both ways but the street was empty apart from a couple of women with prams chatting on the pavement.

'Maggie, Lover Boy is home.'

Maggie dropped the phone and turned. 'How did you get in?'

'How do you think, with my key, sweetheart.' Wredd dangled a bunch of keys from tanned fingers and stepped towards her. 'No welcome home hugs?'

Maggie pushed him away. 'This isn't what we agreed.'

Wredd walked around the room picking up magazines, putting them down, running his hand over the TV.

'What are you doing here, Wredd?'

He sat on the sofa and sprawled himself across the cushions. He tapped a space beside him.

'Come. Sit. Let me tell you about my adventures.'

Maggie sat on the chair opposite and dug her fingernails into the palms of her hands.

'I could do with a drink.' Wredd smiled. 'I've been looking forward to a welcome home cuppa with my pretty wife. What do you say?'

Maggie noticed the softness of his suede jerkin, the shine of his shoes, and the crispness of his white shirt. With the top three buttons open, she could see his tanned skin was adorned with a heavy gold chain.

Wredd pulled the jewellery into view. 'Like it? Dubai has lots of lovely trinkets. I'll show you when I unpack.'

'You're not staying.'

'I do believe I am.' Wredd grinned. 'This cock of the walk has come home to roost. Second thoughts, why don't we skip the coffee and you can give me a rub down in the shower. It's been a long trip.'

Maggie stood looking at him. 'Are you suffering from amnesia? You don't live here anymore. Get out, Wredd. Get out before Stacey comes back.'

Wredd slipped off his jacket and picked up a dark leather

briefcase. He held the case high. 'This, love, is a bonus from MacIntosh for a job well done, you not even curious?'

Maggie turned her back on her husband. He walked around and stood close to her. She could smell aftershave, a sickly, heavy stench. For the first time in weeks, Maggie felt a sharp stab in her head, just at the nape of her neck. The pain shot up over her skull and settled at her temples. She rubbed her eyes and frowned.

'You need to go.'

Wredd was already climbing the stairs when the pain took over and Maggie slumped to the floor.

Chapter 7

Bernice was on the first available ferry back to the mainland. She stood at the café bar and picked at the skin around her fingernails until they bled.

It was Liam who called.

'I'm not sure, Bernice. Stacey's in a right state. Yes, the Infirmary.'

Bernice licked her parched lips as she opened her purse to pay the steward. He leaned over the counter.

'Not found your sea legs? You might be better with a coffee?'

Bernice shrugged. 'I'm fine.'

'Look pale as a pint from the Dairy.' The steward smiled.

'My friend has taken ill. I thought the brandy would steady my nerves. Not sure what I'm walking into when I get there.'

'Best keep your wits about you then.' He paused.' So what's it to be, Cognac or Cappuccino?'

Bernice felt herself relax as she smiled back. 'Cappuccino.' She paused. 'With a dash of Cognac.' They settled into easy conversation, discussing the shipping forecast, jam recipes and Bernice's mock surprise that sea-horses were real but unicorns weren't.

'Baptism of fire was it?' he asked.

Bernice stared at the steward. She thought of Granny's cremation.

'You moving here, fancy a change from the city?' His face creased, eyes the colour of jellied eels stared into hers.

'I grew up on the island.'

'You don't look the type.'

'What type would that be?'

'Well, it's a hard life working the land and you don't strike me as one who would relish the Harvest Festivals?'

'My soul feeds off that land.' Bernice heard the words as though spoken by another.

'Your life a bit tapsalteerie? 'The steward suggested.

'Eh?'

'Topsy-turvy, upside down?' he explained. 'Not to worry. Always hope.' He slid a tea towel towards her, turned and left the galley just as the ramps began to lower. Heavy chains unravelled to expose eager motorists anxious to drive onto the slipway. Bernice noticed a Tarot card poking from beneath the towel and pulled it into view. She recognised the artwork: The Wheel of Fortune. Bernice knew this meant that change in her life was imminent. But what change, and how did the steward know?

Thoughts drifted through her mind like scattered confetti as Bernice looked towards dry land. MacIntosh stood outside the port ticket office waving up at her.

Maggie crushed the plastic cup in her hand.

Chapter 8

Bernice faltered outside the hospital and glanced at the people around her, snaking towards the revolving glass door that would swallow them up and throw them into an anaesthetic world of grief and hope. An old man shuffled along supporting himself with a Zimmer frame. Pale tulips hung limply from a polythene bag over his wrist. He stopped beside Bernice and wheezed heavily.

'You okay?' Bernice asked.

'I'm 82, you know. I swear this hill gets steeper every day.'

Bernice glanced down and noticed that he was wearing slippers. The man caught her gaze.

'These are the only things that I can get my feet into; bunions, gout, arthritis, I've copped the lot.' He laughed. 'I'm unravelling, like the wife's knitting but got to keep my pecker up for the Missus.' He took a deep breath and leaning heavily on the Zimmer frame, pushed forward with the crowd.

It was a tight fit in the waiting area. Bernice wondered whether this was a sign that the visitors were keen to visit or simply keen to get their duty over with.

'Looked like death yesterday.' A short, thin woman spoke to her companion.' Never thought he'd make it through the night, but here we are again.'

'Aye,' the companion agreed. 'Just as well we've got the free bus ticket.'

A small boy stared at Bernice over his father's shoulders. His eyes were pink and puffy.

His father patted his back intermittently, using slow, rhythmic strokes. 'It's all right, Son, Mummy will be home soon.'

'I won't come up,' MacIntosh said from the corridor.

Bernice had forgotten that MacIntosh drove her to the hospital. He reached out. She pulled her arm away.

'Thanks for the lift.' Moving towards the elevators the crowd mulled around making small talk, watching the lights record the progress of the lifts as they moved up and down the shaft with all the groans and moans of a system well past its best.

Bernice desperately wanted to see Maggie but part of her was glad of the diversion as the crowd gradually dispersed via alternative routes.

'I'll wait in the café.' MacIntosh waved a spindly hand towards Bernice as she stepped into the lift.

Bernice sniffed uncomfortably as she squeezed between her fellow passengers.

'Which floor?' A boy had taken charge of the buttons and smiled with youthful enthusiasm. The woman with him glared and muttered under her breath, 'It's not a computer game, Dylan. Just press them all.'

The boy hit each button and spent the rest of the journey staring at his feet.

* * *

Maggie lay unmoving on the bed. Stacey was sitting on a plastic chair by her side, with Wredd standing by the window.

'You sit here, two visitors at a time.' He pulled out a second chair. 'I'll go grab a coffee. Anyone want anything?'

Stacey shook her head.

'Nothing for me thanks. MacIntosh is down there. I suppose you sent him to collect me.' Bernice put her bag on the floor, lifted it onto the bed, and then finally rested it on her lap.

Wredd nodded then left as quickly as snow melting in the sun.

'How are you?' Bernice reached for Stacey's hand.

Stacey shrugged.

'What are the doctors saying?'

'Keep taking tests. I can't get to speak to anyone who'll tell us anything.'

Maggie lay, eyes closed, her breathing soft and low.

'Has she been like this the whole time?' Bernice paled.

Stacey nodded. 'They said she's comfortable. Just babbled clichés, that's all we can get out of them.'

Bernice brushed a stray hair from Maggie's forehead. 'I suppose it takes time but I'm sure she's in the right place.'

Stacey shrugged again.

'Has Wredd spoken to anyone?'

'I never even knew he was back. Just called me to say Mum was in an ambulance. I don't know what happened.'

'But it wasn't anything, you know, like your mum and Wredd argue a lot, but he didn't do anything to cause this. Did he?'

Stacey stared at Bernice and shook her head.

'I know they've had their differences, but he would never hurt her.'

Bernice nodded. 'It'll be those headaches – migraine? I'm sure she just needs a change of medication.'

Wredd arrived back. 'MacIntosh says he'll wait in the car for us, Stacey. Nick's on his way up.'

'I'll go now,' Stacey said." I've been here most of the day. You stay, Bernice. I'm allowed to come out-with the usual visiting hours.'

'How come?' Bernice asked.

'Family only,' Stacey replied.

As Wredd and Stacey walked away, Bernice sagged into the chair. She was rummaging through her handbag as Nick arrived.

'Here.' Nick pulled a tissue from a box on the bedside cabinet. Bernice sniffed.

'What are they saying?' Nick asked quietly.

'No diagnosis, so no prognosis, far as I know.'

'Why are you so upset then?'

'Something Stacey said about family. Hit me hard, Nick, Maggie's as near to family as I've got.'

'Stacey's young. She's upset. That girl loves you like a mother.' Nick rubbed Bernice's shoulder.

'She has a mother.' Bernice buried her face in the tissue.

'Look us all falling out won't help.' He leaned across and kissed Maggie lightly on the cheek. She didn't move. 'I'm sure it's just a bug, a virus, nothing she won't pull out of.'

'Did you see those two morons on your way up?'

Nick nodded.' The Chuckle brothers are back.'

'Stacey said Wredd was with Maggie. He called the ambulance?' Bernice twisted her hands.

'As far as I know he did.'

'But why was he with Maggie? She swore it was over.'

'No idea. Maybe they were trying to talk things through? Patch things up?'

Bernice pulled a handful of tissues from the box and moved closer to Nick. 'It was over, Nick. It was well and truly over. He comes back looking like a reject from a '70s movie and suddenly Maggie's unconscious?'

'I don't like the guy any more than you do but we can't start throwing accusations around. Why don't I run you home? We can stop at the bar for some dinner?'

A muffled bell sounded, announcing the end of visiting.

Maggie snored softly.

'No. Thanks. I just want to get back to the flat. I have a lot of thinking to do.'

Nick stacked the chairs. 'You back for good?'

Bernice looked across at Maggie. 'I'm back for a while. I still have business on the island.'

Neither had much to say as they walked together down the main corridor.

A man in a dark overcoat looked over the rim of his newspaper. As he watched them head towards the exit, he thought that Bernice moved with elegant ease. Her tear stained face added a vulnerability to her beauty. Her fragility made him long even more to touch her.

Chapter 9

Dermott and Robbie set about getting back to work on the farm. Although they didn't breed livestock, they still had a few animals to care for. It was mainly livery work with other folk's horses that kept the money coming in.

'She left suddenly?' Robbie asked.

'That friend of hers has taken ill,' Dermott replied. 'The Maggie one.'

'I liked the Maggie one.' Robbie hauled bales of hay with ease.

'We're not safe yet, Robbie. Berna…Bernice says she's coming back. I don't know where that leaves us.'

'But, she's a woman. She can't run the farm? Why does she want to kick us out? What is it she thinks we ever done?'

'Nothing.' Dermott sighed. 'We've done nothing wrong.'

The two men threw their weight behind the day's work until darkness fell.

* * *

Dermott and Robbie glanced around as they entered Clancy's watering hole. Their estranged father, Tam McShane, sat on his usual bar stool supping his usual ale. His skin had a yellow tinge; his lips were chapped and dry. He coughed and swallowed the phlegm.

'He is disgusting. I'm going for a pee,' Dermott said as he handed Robbie a twenty-pound note. 'The usual for me, ta.'

It was a quiet night with five or six regulars draped around the bar, while one obviously under-age couple, cradling half pints of cider, sat giggling in a corner. McShane licked the froth from a fresh pint and scratched the stubble on his chin. 'Cheers son!' He raised his glass as Dermott walked towards Robbie at the bar.

Robbie handed Dermott what little change was left from the round of drinks. He fiddled with the collar of his shirt. 'I couldn't say no.'

'I could've, dead easy.' Dermott took his drink over to a table.

'Come on, boys, over here with the men. Fancy a game of pool?' McShane called.

Dermott ignored him. Robbie hesitated between the two and clutched his beer with both hands looking from one to the other. Dermott beckoned his brother to join him.

McShane rose and slapped Robbie lightly on his back before resting his arm across his son's shoulder. He whispered in Robbie's ear. 'Keep your old Dad company will you?'

Dermott pushed back his chair and stepped forwards. McShane raised his palms to face his eldest. 'Okay. Okay. Not tonight. But blood's thicker than water. I'm here when you want to talk.' He sat down, his shoulders heaving as another bout of harsh coughing hit him.

Dermott guided Robbie to a chair. Robbie shifted in his seat. He pulled at his shirt collar and as he raised the beer to his mouth his hands were trembling. Dermott rested his elbows on the table and leaned forwards. 'Stay away from him. I'd rather have poison in my veins than any blood of his.'

Robbie sucked the drink and nodded.

'You do know what he did to Bernice?'

Robbie frowned. Dermott grabbed his sleeve. 'Robbie? He should have gone down for that. She was fifteen, for fucksake.'

Robbie sniffed. 'I miss the old man. Not him.' He jerked his head towards McShane. 'Grandad would sort this out.'

Dermott sighed and drained his glass. 'Right, get that down you and we'll head home.'

'Home you say?' McShane stood behind Robbie smirking.' Not for much longer by all accounts eh? That slut'll take the farm even if she has to burn it to the ground.'

'Go wait outside, Robbie.' Dermott saw that everyone barring

the teenage couple had shifted closer, hoping for some entertainment. Robbie didn't move. He sat with his head down, his
shoulders stooped.

'Robbie? Did you hear me?'

Robbie got to his feet quickly and left.

'Aw what the...?' A man rushed across the room wielding a
bar towel. 'Chicken liver's sprung a leak.'

Laughter rang out as Robbie hurried towards the front door
clutching his damp crotch. Dermott threw his car keys. 'Wait in
the van.'

Robbie turned to pick up the keys. His face was flushed, his
eyes pooled with tears. Then he was gone.

'So, big man, is this you going to square up against your own
kin?' McShane wheezed.

Dermott looked at him slowly from head to toe. McShane's
jacket was threadbare, with two buttons missing, the collar of his
shirt frayed and stained. Dermott smiled at the sight of his boots.
One held together with Gaffa tape to keep the sole from flapping.

'What you smiling at?' McShane straightened up and spat on
his hands, rubbed them together then clenched his fists in a
boxer's pose.

'Come on then,' he jeered, jutting his chin towards Dermott,
'give it your best shot.'

Dermott threw some coins to the floor. 'Go buy some soap.'

As he reached the exit, Dermott turned to see McShane scram-
bling on his knees, scraping pennies from the tiles.

Chapter 10

Bernice walked around her flat checking that everything was in the same place as before she left to go to the island for Granny's funeral two weeks earlier. Hex curled his tail around his mistress's, ankles and purred. She made a mental note to hand in a token of thanks to her neighbour. Hex's dishes were clean and the cat looked healthy and content. Bernice felt pleased that there were people in her life that she could trust. She thought of the Wiccan Rede and recited the words in her head.

"Bide within the Law you must, in perfect Love and perfect Trust.

Live you must and let to live, fairly take and fairly give."

A small pile of letters sat on the kitchen table, along with a Post-it note letting Bernice know there was fresh milk in the fridge and bread rolls in the cupboard. She flicked through the letters as she waited for the kettle to boil. Dropping all but one, she ripped the envelope open. As the kettle steamed, Bernice stared at the words.

"I know where your son is."

Bernice shook her head. 'What?' she cried aloud.

Her suitcase sat on the floor. Bernice emptied her handbag. Ferry Tickets. She hadn't dreamt it. Who was sending these letters and why?

Ignoring the click of the kettle, Bernice uncorked a bottle of Merlot and carried it, together with a goblet, into the lounge. Hex was already settled at the foot of the sofa. Bernice closed the curtains and took a long sip of wine. She smoothed an altar cloth on the low table and spread Tarot cards along the length of it. Candles were lit in all corners of the room and a tiger eyed melting pot scattered the scent of Bergamot.

Bernice was determined to make sense of this latest correspondence. She turned each of the cards with hope that fate would deal her a hand that she found healing rather than hurtful.

Sipping the wine as she contemplated their significance in her pursuit to find out what had happened to her son, Humiel, Bernice felt calm and confident.

Her first choice was the Six of Cups, *representing happiness and joy coming from the past. New friendships, ventures and knowledge were all possible with this card.* The second, The Hanged Man: *Spiritually wise and prophetic, the conquest of the worldly.* As she revealed the third card, Bernice shivered. The Five of Swords, *showing failure and defeat as possibilities, with injustice and cowardliness perhaps appearing.* This was not one of her favourites. The fourth card wasn't much better, The Emperor reversed, *which signified immaturity and loss of control.*

Bernice thought of Liam. She sipped at her wine and continued to pluck the last few cards. The High Priestess, *representing knowledge, truth, and an awareness of what lies beneath the surface.* The Moon Reversed, *the containment of imagination by the practical. Peace will be known, but at a price. Risks of any kind should not be taken.* The World, *the card that represents success in all its forms, liberation from want and a celestial consciousness.* Ten of Wands Reversed, *showing that intrigue, separation and loss are possible.* Bernice thought of how that Ten of Wands reversed hung over her past and sipped at her wine once more. She paused before choosing the final card and adding it to the spread in front of her. Seven of Swords, *indicating her plans may fail and that distrust and dishonesty were possible, and no guarantee of success in her quest.*

Bernice lingered over the cards, one by one, absorbing the message that they gave her. She knew she needed to decide whether to follow the signs for her path or consider the changes and alternatives that the reading showed.

Chapter 11

Wredd unpacked. He shoved Maggie's dresses to one side of the wardrobe and hung up his new clothes. Music drifted from Stacey's bedroom. So what if the Liam lad wanted to stay here for a while? Wredd knew that puppy love would run its course.

'I've no problem with that,' he assured Stacey when the suggestion was made.

'I knew you'd be okay about it.'

Wredd smiled. Brownie points for him.

The bed was covered with a white, lace duvet and pile of pink frilled cushions. Wredd threw the cushions to the floor.

'This is not a lady's boudoir, Wifey. Your man is home.' Wredd lay on his back, his hands behind his head and stared at the ceiling. When the phone rang he pressed the speaker button.

'Mac, my man, how lovely to hear from you.'

'So she let you back into the bosom of the family, eh?'

'She's no choice really, must have freaked her out though.'

'I heard. How long they keeping her in?'

'Hopefully, long enough for me to have a chat with batty Bernice and slick Nick. Seems they've been away on a trip together. All three of them.'

'Ménage Trios?'

Wredd laughed. 'With Maggie? More like necrophilia with numpties. Seriously!'

Stacey tapped the bedroom door. 'Dad, are you coming down for something to eat?'

'Sure I am, Princess. Be down in ten.' Wredd paused. 'Listen, Mac. I've got things in hand. We'll meet up tomorrow? Nick's bar sounds good to me. Say two o'clock.'

Ending the call, Wredd leapt to his feet and punched the air.

'I feel good!' he sang. 'Like I knew that I would!' He went downstairs to join his daughter in the kitchen.

'You're looking tired, petal,' Wredd said.

Liam draped his arm protectively across Stacey's shoulder. 'I'll take care of her.'

'Make sure you do. So, what are your plans?' Wredd sat at the head of the table as Stacey laid out bowls of salad, platters of cold meat and jars of pickles. Liam carved thick slices from a crusty loaf.

'Juice is fine.' Wredd nodded as Stacey lifted a carton from the fridge. The three sat down to eat.

'So,' Wredd buttered a slice of bread, 'what was the island trip all about?'

Liam fiddled with the salad servers.

'It was a family thing, Bernice's family. Someone died,' Stacey said quietly.

'Died? Like who? How?'

'Oh it was Bernice's granny.'

Liam lifted lettuce with the servers, dropped some onto his plate and reached for the meat platter.

'Never knew she kept in touch with that granny of hers. Still, she's probably glad the old witch has gone.'

Liam dropped the platter. Slices of meat slithered in all directions some curling on the floor. Stacey bent down to help him clear the mess. She touched Liam's wrist. He pulled away.

'Spilled milk, Son, Stacey'll clear it.' Wredd slapped Liam on the back. 'What say I treat us all to pizza?' He reached for the phone.

'She was a diamond,' Liam said.

Wredd held the phone in mid-air. 'Who was a diamond?'

'Turns out Liam and Bernice are related, Dad.'

Wredd pulled a handful of fast food take away menus from a drawer and tossed them onto the table. 'Never told me that when you asked to move in.'

'Does it make a difference?' Stacey asked.

Wredd paused. 'So what's the relationship between you then?'

'It's complicated,' Liam replied.

Wredd watched as Stacey covered Liam's hand with hers.

'Is it as complicated as the choice between Italian and Chinese? How about some kofta? You ever visited Greece, Liam?'

Liam shook his head.

'Hi, yeah, that's right, a king-size snack box,' Wredd spoke into the phone. 'Sure all the extras.' Wredd gave the address and re-joined the young couple. 'Twenty minutes tops they said. We'll have a culinary cruise around the world. What do you say, Son?'

'I'm not your son.'

Stacey quickly wiped the table, laid out clean cutlery and topped the glasses up with fresh apple juice. 'Leave it, Dad. Liam was close to the old lady.'

'And old man,' Liam snapped.

Wredd stood up quickly. 'Hold on, Tonto, that's my daughter you're screeching at. What's wrong with you? Don't you like having teeth?'

Stacey stood between them. 'Please. Mum's in hospital or had you forgotten?'

'That doesn't excuse this toe-rag from mouthing off.'

'Just don't talk about my family.' Liam pulled himself to his full height.

'But they sound so interesting. What old man? You said...and the old man?'

'Dad, can we talk later. I'm not hungry now. We're going up to the hospital. Are you coming?'

'I'll go in the morning.' Wredd threw a couple of banknotes onto the table.' Get her some grapes or chocolate or something.'

'Maggie's still unconscious, "nil by mouth",' Liam said. 'Don't think she'll have much of an appetite.'

'So? Keep the nurses sweet.'

Stacey hurried to get her coat zipped. She was already in the hallway. Wredd grabbed Liam's arm. 'You won't be here long.' He squeezed. 'Bad news that Bernice, and whatever your link, that makes you bad news, too.'

Later, as Wredd flicked through TV channels, he poked at the remains of the snack box: donner kebab meat curled in stodgy clumps, soggy pakora lay glued to the cardboard. Wredd dripped chilli sauce over the mess. 'Little liar, Liam. Your time will come. You're messing with the wrong man, son.'

He squashed the savoury leftovers with a fork and laughed.

Chapter 12

Bernice called Mrs McEwan from the hospital cafe. The phone rang out longer than usual. The sound of a man's voice answering her call surprised Bernice.

'Village store.'

'Oh hello, is Mrs McEwan there?'

'Who wants to know?'

Bernice looked at her watch. 'Look is she there or not?'

She heard a muffled exchange and Mrs McEwan came on the line. 'Hello, Post Mistress McEwan speaking.'

'It's only me. You got your man covering for you again? What would the Grand Postmaster have to say about that?'

'Bernice.' Mrs McEwan swiped a carrier bag at her husband. He avoided the blow and headed outside. 'What do you want?'

'No "How may I help?"'

'Look. I've offered my help. You seem hell bent on ignoring me.'

'Tsk, tsk, such language, from a good church going woman like yourself. I'm shocked.'

Mrs McEwan ground her teeth at the other end of the line. 'You know full well I like help with the flowers.'

'I'm merely making a courtesy call to let you know I'll be staying here in Glasgow a bit longer.'

'Stay as long as you like. I'm sure Dermott and Robbie can manage well enough without you.'

'Charming. Actually, I wondered if you could get a message to Dermott.'

'Course I will. Send him a letter.'

'Funny. I appreciate some of you linger in the Dark Ages, refusing to embrace modern technology, but I need to speak to him as a matter of urgency.'

The line was quiet.

'Are you still there?'

'Oh, I'm here. Why don't you leave the boys alone? Live your life and let them live theirs. Robbie's taking things hard. He's still in mourning mind.'

'He's mourning, the loss of *my* family?'

'I'll let Dermott call from here.'

'Of course you will. Make sure you get a good listen in. '

'You want him to call or not?'

'You have my number. Let's say about six tonight?' Bernice hung up.

Mrs McEwan stared at the handset before slamming it onto the cradle.

'Keep an eye on the shop!' she called out as she left.

* * *

Later that day Stacey sat with Bernice in her flat.

'You love that cat, don't you?' Stacey asked.

Bernice looked at Hex in a way that suggested she loved her cat more than any human. But then, Hex was more than just a cat. Hex was her confidant.

'My Smugglebums.' Bernice stroked his fur.

Hex turned to look at his mistress. The two held each other's gaze for a few seconds.

'Did you know, Stacey, that in pre-Victorian times animals were deemed to possess no soul and were, for all practical purposes, of a much lesser value than mankind, the supposedly superior being on this planet.'

Stacey shrugged. 'Sure. I read that book you gave me last year. *"Many thought the cat to be a familiar and disguise of witches; the black cat as the witches' familiar being evil and bringing bad luck".*'

Bernice took the cold mug from Stacey. 'Whilst more modern myths in America and Europe, hail if a black cat walks towards you it brings good fortune, only if it walks away, it takes the luck with it.'

'That right?' Stacey asked.

'I prefer myths that value the animal, like in China, the cat – Mao – is a symbol of clairvoyance, linked to the moon and to everything that characterizes it.'

Hex continued to stare at Bernice, sensing when his mistress was on a roll.

'Muslims thought the cat a lucky animal with seven lives, and that a black cat had magical powers, that right?' Stacey asked. 'Or was it nine lives?'

'You really did read the book. I believe Hex has the power of second sight.' Bernice smiled.

Stacey grabbed Bernice's wrist. 'Mum needs your help. Don't you think?'

'And she'll get all the help I can give.'

'What about this Wiccan stuff, the magic, you and Hex. You must be able to do something?' Stacey's grip tightened, 'Please Bernice.'

Hex purred and settled at Stacey's feet.

Bernice sat beside Stacey and held her hand. 'I thought you understood. It's not proper to cast a healing spell for someone without their asking for help.'

Stacey pushed Bernice's hand away but Bernice intertwined their fingers. 'Let me finish. It's important not to violate someone else's belief system, but under circumstances like this, I'll do my best.'

Stacey relaxed back on the sofa.

'But,' Bernice continued, 'we don't know yet what caused Maggie to collapse. I can, and I will, visit every day. I'll do my best but I can't change the path of the Universe.'

Stacey shrieked. 'So what are you saying? You're all candles and crystals but when it comes down to it, you can't actually DO anything to help!'

'Stacey. If it were that simple to heal, to cure, do you imagine that there would be so much suffering in the world?'

'I don't care about the world. I just want my mum back in good health.'

Bernice cradled Stacey in her arms and let her cry. She brushed a damp strand of hair from Stacey's face. 'It's the old fate debate Stacey. Are some things down to fate, or just coincidence? Like Wredd coming home and your mum falling ill so suddenly.'

Stacey pushed Bernice away and grabbed her jacket and bag.

'You're such a fraud! Just because your family are all weirdos doesn't mean mine are. Mum's obviously been ill for a while now. Some friend you are! Too busy wrapped up in your own Home Movie drama to think about anyone else.'

She left abruptly, banging the front door closed as she went.

Hex stretched. Bernice stroked the cat. 'What a mess, Hex. What a mess.'

Chapter 13

Bernice stood at her window and watched Stacey hurry along the road. There was no easy answer. Why did people mistake the power of magic for the fabrications of optical illusions, performed on stage for fickle entertainment?

Having showered, Bernice sat for a few minutes in meditation. She wanted to clear her emotions, stabilise her chakras.

She preferred to practise her craft in isolation, mainly because she was never one to seek groups to affiliate with in any area of her life. She enjoyed the primary benefit of being a Wicca solitary for its complete openness, serving only her deities, leaving her free to practice however she saw fit. It was a freedom that left her able to perform rituals spontaneously, although some might think she did so in an unorthodox manner, her intentions were always good.

As she matured and developed away from the restraints of the island, Bernice recognised that Granny's influence was what made her feel complete. Had she been privileged to share her adult years with Granny, there would, she was convinced, have been many hours of discussion about Bernice's ancestry, way further back than any birth certificate could show. There was a time in her twenties when Bernice moved towards a Coven, and indeed was initiated within one. But her devotion was tested following a string of disillusionments, when some members started charging for services that Bernice strongly felt should be offered in the spirit of goodwill, as she believed herself fortunate to have her own spiritual gifts bestowed upon her. She did, however, continue to meet with other witches within circles at the Sabbatts.

Bernice lifted a small wand from her altar. She had crafted the tool from a fallen branch of a Rowan tree many years before. Also known as "The Tree of Life", the Rowan was an ideal source of strong and resilient wood suitable for hand carving. Its old Gaelic name from the ancient Ogham script was "Luis" from which the place name Ardlui on Loch Lomond may have been derived. Bernice spent many hours whittling the wood, smoothing the surface and shaping the wand. She channelled her energies into the wand before decorating with crystals and carvings. The physical characteristics of the Rowan tree include tiny, five pointed stars or pentagrams on each berry, opposite its stalk. This symbol was familiar to Bernice throughout her life and encouraged her to choose the wood. Over the years, Bernice carved various rune symbols on the wand. Her fingers searched the surface. She stroked the carving and hesitantly hovered over the word Nauthiz, meaning free from distress, letting go, releasing the past. This would happen, and soon, she hoped, but for now Bernice's calling was to help Maggie.

Clasping the wand close to her breast, Bernice sighed then placed it gently on her altar cloth, already spread on the table. Bernice energised herself by cleansing her hands and lighting a rose candle and incense. She ran her left hand over her right hand, then her right hand over her left. This she did several times until she felt the energy building. Picking up her wand with the hand she used for writing, she closed her eyes and imagined a stream of silver white light coming from the universe and entering the top of her head. She imagined the light beaming down and coursing along her arm, into her hand, and out from her fingertips. As the beam of light left her fingertips, she felt it going into her wand, felt the energy flowing as she charged her wand with power. The feeling was exhilarating.

Bernice aimed to charge a plant with energy that would alleviate Maggie's suffering. She hoped that the medical staff would have news that would help them both tackle the situation and bring Maggie back to health.

Despite living in a city flat, Bernice claimed an area of the communal back green, much to the bemusement of neighbours, who left her to cultivate whatever herbs, vegetables and flowers she desired. So long as the small allotment didn't cause any obstruction to their wheelie bin shelter, residents, overall, showed no sign of concern.

Some showed a little interest, others pretended to, but the majority just ignored the patchwork of nature's wonders as they hurried through their busy lives. Bernice's proposal for a chicken run and beehive was, however, met with a majority objection.

Bernice wanted to focus on a plant that would have meaning for Maggie. Of course, she could uproot and re-pot some bluebells, not only beautiful but magical, closely linked to the realm of fairies and sometimes referred to as "fairy thimbles." In order to call fairies to a convention, the bluebells would be rung. Whichever plant she chose, Bernice needed to be polite to the energies (devas) that inhabit plants. She knew never to pick without asking and to always explain the reason why the cutting was needed.

Bernice knew it was never good to offer white flowers to a sick person. Better to offer those with a red bloom, as red represented healthy, red blood cells and life. She considered poppies; synonymous with sleep and rest, but also with war. She thought of roses, but Maggie and Bernice's relationship was not based on romance.

Another thought slipped into her mind – what if the hospital didn't allow plants or flowers on the wards? Hadn't she heard someone say that recently?

Bernice always kept herbs drying, and looking in her airing cupboard, she selected a few favourites that might help, but realistically, without a diagnosis, Bernice could only address Maggie's spiritual health.

Another thought struck her: apples. Surely the NHS hadn't banned apples? Packed with vitamins! Nosey nurses wouldn't notice that when you cut an apple in half it reveals the five pointed star that is the Wiccan emblem of protection.

Bernice cast a circle of protection in her living room by standing in the middle of where she wanted said circle to be. She relaxed and breathed deeply. In Bernice's imagination, the top of her head opened up like a funnel to receive divine, white light. She spread her arms wide, palms facing out. With each inhalation of breath, Bernice visualised that she was pulling down pure, divine light through the crown of her head, and as she breathed out, she channelled this light out through her palms to create a protective shield around her. As she filled the space about her with this high-vibration energy, Bernice experienced a tingling sensation and felt light and uplifted.

Holding one arm outstretched and pointing to the edge of the circle, she spun around clockwise three times, mentally marking out her circle with the divine light. Raising her arms above her head, she invited the deities to bless the circle, to free and protect her whilst she cast the spell for Maggie.

Finally, Bernice pointed her wand towards a ripe apple, and that was it, deal done.

Feeling positive, Bernice set about preparing for another hospital visit.

Chapter 14

In the visitors' waiting room at the infirmary, Bernice clutched a hessian bag of apples. Her beauty and elegance had not gone unnoticed by a gang of builders working nearby. Several comments were launched in her direction, followed by a gaggle of schoolboy squeals as a young apprentice was terrorised into approaching her. He looked no older than Liam and as he reached where she was sitting, she felt a strong maternal urge to hug his trembling frame. The boy wiped his hands on his overalls.

'My workmates have dared me to come over and speak to you. I'm an apprentice. I'm really sorry. It's an initiation thing,' he squeaked. Sweat was building on his upper lip. He licked it away.

'I've never had a girlfriend, and they're egging me on to chat to you.' He stumbled and hit his knee on a corner of the low table between them. 'I wouldn't. I mean I would. I mean I'm a lot younger than you. You're really good looking. Not old at all. I wouldn't even ask. I just…' The boy looked on the verge of tears.

Bernice glanced across at the workmen. They had piled themselves onto various levels of scaffolding and were watching with keen interest. She sat upright threw a hand to her chest, tossed her hair back and gave a girlish giggle.

'Sit beside me.' She lifted her handbag off the chair and the boy sat down. She could almost smell his virginity and barely stopped herself from counting the freckles on his face. 'Smile, and pretend that we're in conversation. Who's that bruiser with the double belly?'

'Lucky,' the boy mumbled.

'Well,' Bernice purred. 'His luck's just run out. 'See that newspaper tucked inside his jeans? You leave that here, under this seat, when your shift finishes.'

'But he's got all his horses marked out on it.'

'He's a gambler eh? Maybe a grown man like that, or should I say, overgrown, shouldn't make bets on other people's destiny. You'll find a way. Just get it for me, and the can he's drinking from.'

They heard a loud whistle and cheer as Bernice leaned towards the boy. She rested her hand on his shoulder.' I know this may seem strange but let's just do as I ask. If you do, I can assure you that lot will never bother you again with their bullying.'

'It's just banter. They don't mean any harm.'

'So are you feeling the fun factor?'

The boy looked down at his feet and shook his head. Bernice titled his chin upwards and kissed him lightly on both of his smooth cheeks, just enough to leave an imprint of ruby-red lipstick.

'Seriously, leave the newspaper and drinks can here and I promise, tomorrow will be an altogether different day for you.'

The boy scratched his head and wandered back to be engulfed by a swarm of backslapping men intent on his humiliation.

* * *

Maggie looked rested but pale. Her hands lay unnaturally folded over the bedcover. Bernice noticed that she wore no rings and her normally polished fingernails had been scrubbed bare.

'Maggie?' There was no response as Bernice placed her apple offering beside her friend. 'Maggie?' she tried again.

Maggie lay still, like Sleeping Beauty awaiting her prince.

'She's been out all day.' The patient in the next bed confirmed. 'Don't know why she isn't in intensive care.'

'Why would she be?'

'If she's in a coma like some say?'

'She's just sleeping.'

'Must be dead beat. Still, better than being dead, eh?'

As the old woman's visitors approached, she turned her attention towards them and Maggie and Bernice were forgotten.

Bernice unclipped a folder from the end of Maggie's bed. She flipped through the A4 pages fastened to it. Apart from Maggie's name and date of birth, none of it made any sense. A young curate approached her. Bernice smiled.

'Friend or family?' the curate asked.

'Best friend, as close as family,' Bernice replied.

The curate was clutching a bible and handed Bernice a credit card sized print of a psalm.

'Hospital visitor.' He held out his hand. 'We try to comfort the patients and their relatives, whatever their beliefs.'

Bernice smiled again. 'Thank you. I'll leave this with her.'

'It's a difficult time for all when someone falls ill. May I ask what the problem is with...'

He looked at the board above Maggie's bed. 'Mar-gar-et?'

'I don't know what's wrong exactly. She was having a lot of headaches and now she seems to be asleep most of the time.'

'Ah, sleep in itself can be a great healer. She's in good hands, here in the infirmary, I mean. God bless you both.'

Bernice watched the curate nod and exchange small talk with several patients and visitors, leaving complimentary laminated cards with each of them.

'Who was that?' Stacey asked as she arrived.

'Oh, he's a vicar or priest or something. Isn't it nice that he didn't ask about your mum's beliefs but gave her his blessing regardless?'

'Every little helps.' Stacey fussed over re-arranging Maggie's hair on the pillow. She lifted a water jug from the bedside cabinet.

'It's full,' Bernice said.

'Warm though. I'll get some chilled.'

As Stacey left the ward, Maggie stirred slightly.

'Oh, the mention of a drink and you're on the mend? Fancy

some ice and lemon with it?' Bernice moved closer to test Maggie's reaction.

Maggie didn't move again throughout the visit.

As the bell rang, Maggie and Stacey walked in awkward silence from the ward. Both exhausted at trying to hide their fears and hopes. On arrival at the bus stop, Stacey spoke first.

'Sorry I was off with you that other time.'

'No problem. We're all worried.'

'Dad should've gone to see the consultant today but he missed the appointment.'

'He did what? Why did he miss the appointment?' Bernice spoke louder than she had intended, drawing attention from some of the people in the bus queue.

'He said he was caught up in some business meeting. I didn't know until he never showed up to bring me here.'

'So you didn't get to hear what the consultant had to say either?' Bernice was almost shouting by this point.

'I did phone when I knew Dad wouldn't be here on time but they said they would see him again at visiting.'

'Wredd wasn't at visiting though was he? Obviously more important things to do than look after his wife.'

'I know. I kept hoping he'd show up. Then we could've spoken to someone.'

Bernice was already heading back to the main building.

Stacey called after her. 'They won't tell you anything. Not until they've spoken to Dad. He's her next of kin.'

A bus drew up at the kerb. Several of the people in the queue witnessed their argument. A few nudged each other; some shook their heads whilst others nodded sympathetically. Stacey stood to one side and let the people board. Bernice never looked back.

A man sat on a bench across from the bus stop. He had witnessed the brawl and watched as Stacey paced from the bus stop to the main door and back again. She did this twice, once in a rushed fury and the second time with more hesitance.

Stacey's third attempt saw her disappear behind the sliding doors of the hospital entrance.

The man followed quickly, at a distance, keeping Stacey in his sight.

Chapter 15

Bernice sat in Nick's bar waiting for him. Nick arrived with a pile of brochures in his arms.

'Bernice, always good to see you, how's tricks?' He raised a finger to his lips. 'No offence intended.'

'Offence taken and stored for use at another time.' Bernice pushed a glass towards Nick and poured wine from a bottle on the table. 'What's that you have there, paint charts?'

'So, really, how are things with you? Maggie?'

'I can't get a peep out of the hospital. Apparently King Wredd has to be spoken to first and he's gone missing with Monkey MacIntosh.'

'They'll be planning dodgy deals somewhere. But surely a man wants to know what's wrong with his wife?

'A man would, yes. But we're talking about Wredd and he's more of a weasel.'

'Can't Stacey speak to the doctors?'

'I tried that. She's still pretty young in her ways, and I think she's terrified of what they might say. She won't go without him.'

'Couldn't you go with her?'

Bernice shook her head. 'I tried that too. Poor girl doesn't know what to do and they won't see me on my own. Stupid isn't it? If Maggie didn't have family, would they just not tell anyone what was happening?'

'Expect its protocol or something. Don't suppose you can get a hold of Wredd and persuade him to take you and Stacey along to get the facts first hand.'

Bernice nodded slowly. 'I've so much going on in my life right now. I'm swinging from one emotion to another.'

'All that stuff on the island can't have helped.'

'It's made matters worse. I feel now that I may never know what happened to Humiel. There was always hope before but with McShane being adamant the baby died, I'm torn with what to believe.' Bernice re-filled her glass.

'I don't know what to say except, Liam is a decent lad, Bernice; maybe if you got to know him better it would help.'

'I'm really not sure where Liam fits into all of this. As you say, he's a nice enough lad. But he is not my son and that's who I've been looking for all this time.'

Bernice squeezed her handbag, considering telling Nick about the latest letter.

Nick waved Liam to bring over a fresh bottle. Liam uncorked the wine at the table.

'No,' Bernice said.

'Sorry,' Liam replied.' Is this not what you had before?' He looked at the label. Bernice looked at Nick.

'It's fine. Just leave the bottle. I'll pour,' Nick said.

Liam wiped his hands on his bar apron and went back to the gantry.

'Did you think we could just sit and have a chat over a glass of plonk?' Bernice rasped.

'Not at all, look, he hasn't worked here long but he is honest, punctual and reliable and I know he's well loved up with your Stacey. He's just a young boy, Bernice.'

'It's all too much. I can't even think about where he might sit in my family tree.'

'Doubt it's easy for him either. He lost the two people he saw as parents. Whether they were or not isn't the issue.'

Bernice changed the subject. 'I need to find out what's happening with Maggie. It doesn't look good. I don't know what caused it or even what "it" is?'

'I'll ask around. We'll get Wredd up there. I'm sure it won't be too serious.'

'Nick,' Bernice began.

'What is it?'

'You did have feelings for Maggie?'

'I still do. She isn't going anywhere. She'll be back here in no time, complaining about too much froth on her coffee and her bacon not being crispy enough.'

'I mean.' Bernice paused. 'I mean, when you and Maggie were together. That wasn't just childhood sweetheart stuff was it?'

Nick tapped the tabletop with a beer mat.

'Bernice. We were teenagers. Love, lust, call it what you will. At the time I would've pulled the stars from the sky if she'd asked me to. We're all older and wiser. Let's not think back to the past.'

'You never married.'

'But she did. Maggie did.' Nick tossed a beer mat and it went spinning across the room.

'That anger you did it?'

'What is this, an afternoon of psychobabble? I loved her or at least from all that I knew of love, I loved her. What more do you want me to say?'

'You've stayed close over the years.'

'As friends, I care about her, of course I do and with that idiot she married it's just as well I've been around to give her a shoulder to cry on. What's with the inquisition?'

Bernice sipped her wine.

'Bernice?'

'Best I get home now. Hex will be wondering where I am.' Bernice scraped back her chair.

'Look, let me know how things go. I'll phone you if I track Wredd down.' Nick helped Bernice as she pulled her jacket on. He rested his hands on her shoulders breathing in the scent of her. 'Bernice.'

'Yes?'

She turned to face him.

'I'll always be here for you both, you and Maggie.'

Chapter 16

It was a dull day on the island. Dermott wiped his hands on his jeans.

'Here.' Mrs McEwan handed him a tumbler of whiskey.

Dermott drained the glass with one gulp and held it aloft, expecting another shot.

'Get the call over and done with. Then you can have the bottle.' Mrs McEwan handed the phone to Dermott. 'Don't let her bulldoze you into making any rash decisions.'

'One more.' Dermott reached for the bottle.

'No. Man up! Tell her she can't come back here. What would be the point? There's nothing here for her.'

Dermott cradled his head in his hands. 'Why all the mystery, are we living in some kind of occult? I've never pried Mrs McEwan, but there is something not right with all of this. I know that you and Granny were always brewing up something with your hocus-pocus. You two were always in cahoots with your secrets.'

'We practiced our craft that's all.'

'I remember the lotions, potions and funny notions. I love the land, too. It's how I earn my living, but you two? There must have been more to your carrying on?'

Mrs McEwan tapped the bottle of whiskey. 'You'll never find the answer at the bottom of that. Like father, like son. Is that the path you're going to follow? Dragging that simple brother of yours down with you?'

Dermott thumped his fist hard on the table. 'Don't talk about Robbie like that.'

'Everyone else does. What'll happen to Robbie if you drown your sorrows in whiskey?'

Dermott dialled Bernice's number as Mrs McEwan dithered around the kitchen.

Dermott stood and straightened his shoulders as he prepared for the speech of his life.

'Let her do the talking. Don't agree to anything until we have time to discuss it.' She placed the bottle back in front of him. Dermott rested his hand on the cap and left it there.

'Yes. It's me. Six o'clock like you asked.'

Mrs McEwan strained to make sense of the conversation and wished she could hear what Bernice had to say. Instead, she made do with reading Dermott's body language. His shoulders slumped; his face drained of colour as he knocked the top off and drank the whiskey raw from the bottle.

'Well?' Mrs McEwan asked when he finally replaced the receiver. 'Well?'

'Leave me alone for a bit would you, woman. Leave me alone.'

'I have the right to know.'

'She says she has another letter. Same as before, "I know where your son is". Are you playing games with us all?'

Mrs McEwan shuffled away from him. 'Not me, Dermott. I've had enough of cryptic letters to last me a lifetime. You can sleep here tonight. You'll find blankets under the settee.'

Dermott growled. 'I'll stay a while then head home. Robbie will be looking for me.'

'But...when can we talk about things?' the old woman asked. 'What did she have to say for herself apart from the letter? Is she planning on coming back to the island?'

'Well, this latest note is just giving her more of an excuse, don't you think? Please just go. Leave me in peace. I'll drop the latch on my way out.'

Mr McEwan was in the hallway as his wife left the room. He shook his head.

'Will it never end? Will it never end?' he asked.

He slipped an arm around her shoulders and they climbed the stairs together.

Chapter 17

Wredd was getting ready for his appointment with the consultant.

'To be fair, Dad, Bernice is really worried.'

Wredd straightened his tie and ran a finger down the lapel of his suit jacket.

'Dad? Can she come with us or not?'

'Family only.'

Liam kissed Stacey on the top of her head. 'Go. It's the only way you'll know exactly what they have to say. I'm here for you.'

'You've your own worries.'

'I can still share yours. Without you I'd never have got through all that's happened.'

Wredd called from the doorway, 'Okay, Casanova. Let her go now.'

Liam shrugged as Stacey tried to speak. He placed a finger over her lips. 'Find out what's happening.'

Liam called Bernice. She sounded harassed.

'Is this a bad time?' he asked. 'I wanted to let you know they've another appointment with the consultant.'

'It's never a good time lately. Sorry, yes, thanks for telling me. Maybe I should come over? Be there for when they get home?'

'I don't think that's a great idea.' Liam played with the phone cord, twisting and stretching the coil.

'Not avoiding me are you?' Bernice asked.

'I've a shift at seven. Only wanted to let you know they're away to find out what's going on.'

Bernice heard the strain in his young voice. She imagined him standing alone in a house that wasn't his home. Grieving and longing for the same kind of family love that she herself longed for. Bernice thought of the young apprentice she had met earlier in the week.

'Liam. We do need to talk, you and me. I'm not ready yet because I've so much I need to find out first. I never knew you existed. You came looking for me, so you have the upper hand. Right now though, we need to leave our baggage to one side and look out for Maggie.'

'I know. I really want to be with Stacey. Her dad doesn't seem to like you or me very much.'

'Bernice laughed. 'You mean Wredd? Sure, he's seeing red! Thinks he has control of the women in his life but he can barely control his hair. Have you seen the amount of gel he piles on there, like he isn't slimy enough?'

Liam laughed nervously. 'I'll go then. Stacey did say they might pop into Nick's on the way back. Maybe see you all in there later?'

'You very well might.'

Bernice turned her thoughts to the young apprentice at the hospital. He had completed his task and more. She drew a carrier bag from beside her sofa.

'Newspaper, fizzy drink can and a lovely selection of cigarette butts. Ideal.'

Hex circled his mistress.

'Time to sort out a man with the brains of a goldfish, no offence to goldfish,' Bernice explained. 'Then it's goodbye to another bully and sardines for you.'

Within an hour the spell was cast and Bernice was showered, changed and heading for Nick's bar.

Chapter 18

Bernice settled at the bar.

'Good to see you,' Nick welcomed her. 'Thought you'd be at the hospital?'

'No, Wredd and Stacey are away up, speaking to the consultant. Fingers, toes and everything else crossed, Maggie is going to be okay.'

Nick smiled. ''Course she is, she has us on her side. What you having?'

'A nice, warm, red please.'

Nick passed a large glass of merlot to Bernice. 'Be with you in just a minute.' He nodded to another customer and left to take his order.

Liam was polishing glasses at the other end of the bar. He sneaked a look at Bernice. She sat straight and elegant. Her fingernails matched the deep burgundy in her glass as she trailed her forefinger around the rim. Liam always hated his own coppery mop but the way that the streetlight shone through the window and framed Bernice, she looked almost angelic. Her hair spilled like crystallised coils of candied sugar. Liam noticed that she often wound her hair around her fingers, as if the curls were a comfort blanket. Running his hand through his own hair, he only succeeded in making it spike up even more than usual. He thought his own thatch looked more like a burst mattress. Liam gradually worked his way towards Bernice's end of the bar.

'Is everything okay with you?' he asked.

'I'm waiting for news. You did say that you thought Stacey would stop off here on the way back.'

'I'm sure they will.' Liam wiped the bar top with a cloth. 'Is everything all right back home?'

'Back home on the island you mean?'

'Dermott and Robbie are okay, you know. They've worked

their butts off keeping the farm going.'

'Not theirs to keep though is it?'

Liam took the empty glass that Bernice held out towards him. 'Same again?'

She nodded.

'I came looking for you once we knew how sick Ma was.'

Bernice raised her eyebrows.

'I called her Ma because that's what Dermott and Robbie called her.'

'But she wasn't their Ma, Liam, and I don't think she was yours either. How much do you actually know about your parents, whoever they were or are?'

Nick joined the conversation. 'Go help in the cellar, Liam. That delivery has to be sorted.'

Liam threw down the damp cloth and walked away.

'Come on, Bernice. The poor lad's in a right state as it is. Are you are trying to tip him over the edge?'

'Maybe he knows more than he's letting on?' Bernice took a sip of the wine.

'I doubt it. Never says much, but I get the impression he's heartbroken, whatever his relationship to you or the others. He grew up on the farm. I honestly don't think he knows any more than you do.'

Wredd and Stacey walked into the bar. Stacey looked like she had been crying. Wredd summoned Nick's attention.

'Pint and a whisky chaser for me.' He turned to Stacey. 'What you having my lovely?'

'Strong Polish vodka…and more vodka, with a dash of lemonade.'

Bernice caught her ankle in the strap of her bag as she quickly slid from the barstool. She stumbled against Wredd.

'Steady, girl, I'm a married man, you know.' Wredd swallowed the whisky and winked.

Bernice ignored him and went to Stacey. She placed her hands on Stacey's shoulders.

'What are they saying about Maggie?'

Stacey hesitated, took the tall glass of vodka from Wredd and replied, 'She's going to pull through. They say it's a viral thing but not anything terminal. Not sure if the headaches were a warning or just co-incidence.'

Bernice swept Stacey into her arms. 'Oh, I'm so pleased! Is she conscious? When is she coming home?'

'Slow down,' Wredd interrupted.' She'll be in for a while yet. No rush.'

'Oh, Bernice, where's Liam? I need to let him know what's happening,' Stacey said.

'He's in the cellar. Go find him,' Nick replied.

'So,' Bernice asked, 'what exactly are they saying, Wredd?'

'They said she'll be fine. Apparently needs rest and some TLC. Tender, loving care, like I always give my darling wifey. Maggie's always been an attention seeker.'

'I'll look after her,' Bernice offered. 'I don't need to go back to the island any time soon.'

'She has me and Stacey. You go sort out your own family.' Wredd smirked.

'Come on, you two. This is great news. Can't we just focus on what's best for Maggie?' Nick could sense an argument brewing.

MacIntosh appeared in the bar.

'All we need,' said Bernice.

'Thanks for the welcome.' MacIntosh leaned over to kiss her cheek. Bernice drew her head away from him.

'All's well with Maggie, I hear. Good news. Good news.' MacIntosh ordered a drink.

'You spoke to him before me?' Bernice turned to Wredd.

Wredd and MacIntosh huddled together at the bar and turned their backs to her.

'Go through to the back room,' Nick said. 'I'll be with you in two minutes.'

Bernice walked through to the living quarters on autopilot.

'Okay, guys, I get that Bernice isn't your favourite person, but give her a break would you? Maggie's her friend and she really cares a lot about her.'

Wredd spoke first. 'Maggie's my wife you know, mother of my child.'

MacIntosh laughed quietly. 'Think that's trumps then.' He tapped his glass against Wredd's. 'Cheers!'

'I think you should finish up and leave.' Nick pushed his shoulders back.

'Barred are we?' Wredd asked.

'Don't be here when I get back.' Nick headed for the back room.

Bernice was slumped on the sofa amongst till receipts and promotional drinks posters.

'Bastards,' she said.

' I couldn't agree more.' Nick sat across from her and took her hands in his. 'Forget those two. Maggie's on the mend. That's all that matters.'

Bernice looked Nick in the eye. 'Is it? She gets better, and then what? He's not for leaving her in peace.'

'He is her husband, and as he just reminded me, Stacey's father.'

'No he isn't,' Bernice blurted.

Chapter 19

Back on the island, Mrs McEwan placed the pink vanity case on her bed. The letters inside tied in neat bundles. Dermott was due to meet her at the farm.

Mr McEwan opened the bedroom door slowly. He glanced at the open case and shook his head. Mrs McEwan pushed the letters flat, clipped the bag shut and stood to face her husband. 'It has to be done, whatever the consequences.'

'You'll lose your pension, the shop, everything.' He blocked her exit.

'I know. I should never have kept these from 'aul Mrs Hanlon, but I was scared of her 'aul man. Weren't you?'

'Not so scared as to put our livelihood in danger. We'll lose our home, everything. You could even face a jail sentence.'

Mrs McEwan gripped the bag tighter. 'I don't see it coming to that. I don't see anyone caring that I breached my position as post mistress.'

Mr McEwan stood his ground. 'What would be the point now? After all that's happened? Let it lie. Burn the letters.'

'Not mine to burn.'

'Not yours to hold onto all these years either.' He stepped aside. 'Go. But it'll be the end of everything we've worked for.'

Mrs McEwan hesitated before smudging a kiss on his cheek. She touched his face. 'I can't take this secret to the grave with me.'

He watched his wife go down the stairs and heard the click of the back door as it locked behind her before making his way to the kitchen and setting about producing a pot of tea. He leaned against the kitchen sink waiting for the kettle to boil, looking around him. Same old sofa they had got when they married, and it was second hand then. Crisp, white, cotton covers on each arm, with fat cushions in between. A high back, winged chair sat to the left of the fireplace, a greased patch on the back where he rested his head of an evening. He touched his balding scalp thinking of the fine mop of dark waves that he sported when they first met. He had loved his moustache back then, although now he couldn't face the day without a good hot shave.

Their wedding photo still took up the centre of the mantle, with space at each side. He had built the fireplace not long after they moved here, broad enough to take a cluster of family photographs. Still there was only the one. How he longed for a son to carry on the family name, and Mrs McEwan? He knew motherhood would have been the making of her.

Her knitting box sat beside the armchair opposite his. She still knitted those tiny clothes and shawls. For years, she crafted every stitch with love. Aul' Mrs O'Hanlon and her made a right pair, the two of them clacking away with their needles. He thought them a bit competitive at times but the two women seemed to share an understanding. Mrs O'Hanlon's needlework was exquisite and she stretched her patience explaining the techniques to her companion. They were friends back in the early days. When Bernice was conceived out of wedlock, Mrs McEwan couldn't hide her disappointment. Of course, Aul man O'Hanlon was raging like the proverbial bull, especially when he found out his only daughter was carrying a traveller's child.

The caravans came most years. It was good for the community. A great help with harvesting, and the menfolk didn't spare their cash in Clancy's bar. The women and children kept themselves within the camp mostly. It was a great shame to O'Hanlon when, after the caravans left, his daughter became more and more swollen with the seed of the devil (O'Hanlon's term for his unborn grandchild). Bernice's mother was young and frightened. All the soothing of her own mother couldn't ease her pain as she longed for the caravans to return.

Throughout the pregnancy, O'Hanlon made it clear that any son his daughter bore would be put to good use on the farm. After Bernice was born her mother was often seen down by the shore, looking out to the horizon as though expecting to see her love ride in on the waves to rescue her. The caravans didn't return that first year or the next and after that Bernice's mother lost count. O'Hanlon's attitude never waned. It was said that he uttered not a word to his daughter after the birth. Mrs O'Hanlon was often on Mrs McEwan's doorstep in tears, sharing her worries about her daughter and the baby.

'I don't agree with bearing a child out of wedlock, you know that, but that bairn Bernadette is a joy to be around. It's so sad that your daughter can't embrace motherhood.'

'I think she needs help, maybe on the mainland. I've tried many spells and offered so much to have her mental wellbeing restored. I'm drained. I can do no more.'

Both women were well practised in their spiritual beliefs.

Bernice's mother frequently left the house in the hours of darkness. She said the moonlight soothed her. It was after one such walk that Granny woke to find her daughter had not returned. The villagers frantically searched the woods, the farmland and every hut and barn on the island. There was no trace. It was as though she had simply disappeared. Police were drafted in from the mainland and after weeks of searching, Bernice's mother was pronounced missing presumed drowned.

There could be no other explanation. Could there?

Chapter 20

Mrs McEwan arrived at the farmhouse breathless and thirsty. She stopped to reset the horseshoe above the front door. 'Superstitious I may be, but in my day the shoe must be hung open end down, to keep bad spirits away.' She pushed past Dermott into the cottage.

'I nailed it the other way. Sorry. I thought it held good luck with the open end upwards.'

'Who told you that? The blacksmith, he knows nothing.'

'I found it by the side of the road and he cleaned it up a bit. I think he's okay.'

'The letters you gave Bernice. Has she taken them?' she asked.

'You mean the ones in the old tin? I'm not sure. With the old man passing like that and then the services I don't think there was much time for her to look at them properly.'

Together the two looked around the farmhouse for the biscuit tin Dermott gave Bernice at her granny's funeral. It was a short search. Bernice had taken over the biggest bedroom when she stayed at the farm. Her silk kaftan hung on the back of the door. Inside the wardrobe was a small collection of jeans, t-shirts and two thick jumpers.

'Look in the drawers.' Mrs McEwan instructed Dermott.

He shoved his hands into his pockets. 'Can't you?'

'What?' she asked, her voice muffled as she rummaged through the clothing in the wardrobe.

'Sure, her own drawers might be in there and I have no desire to be touching lady things.'

'Lady things?' Mrs McEwan laughed. 'No wonder you're still a bachelor. Move aside.'

Dermott lay on the floor and peered under the bed, anxious to avert any possible sighting of Bernice's undergarments.

'It's here!' He grunted as he banged his head on the bedframe.

Dermott reached further under the bed sliding his body along the wooden floor. His hair caught on a spring.

'Bring it out then.'

'I'm stuck.' He winced as the spring tangled deeper into his hair.

'In the name...' Mrs McEwan grabbed his boots and pulled as hard as she could. Dermott yelped and slid the tin out first. He sat rubbing his head as Mrs McEwan opened the lid.

'Sit here, you big drip.' Mrs McEwan was sitting on the bed with both the old biscuit tin and vanity case beside her.

'It doesn't feel right,' Dermott said, still rubbing his scalp.

'Does it feel right that you and Robbie may be thrown into the street?'

'She hasn't actually said she wants us out.'

'She hasn't actually said she doesn't. How long is she away for?'

'Not sure.' Dermott contorted his body trying to catch a glimpse of the back of his head in the dresser mirror.

'What else did she say when you spoke on the phone?'

'Said her friend Maggie was ill, she was staying in Glasgow until she got well and that she would be back. I swear I never knew anything about what happened to Bernice or her baby.'

'You haven't told anyone else about finding this tin have you?'

Dermott shook his head.

'Right then, let's get these in some sort of order and see if we can make any sense of it all.'

Chapter 21

When Stacey walked into the back room of the bar with Liam, Nick was still staring at Bernice, trying to understand the implications if Wredd wasn't Stacey's biological father.

'What do you mean?' Stacey asked Bernice. 'You said, "No he isn't" who isn't what?'

Bernice turned quickly. 'She, as in your mum, Maggie, isn't going to take long to recover. I'm sure of that. Not with us lot all rallying round.'

Stacey looked at Nick. He was still staring at Bernice.

'Yes,' he said. 'She's a real fighter your mum.'

Liam noticed the awkwardness between Bernice and Nick and saw from Stacey's expression that she had too.

'Can you go home with Stacey?' Liam asked Bernice. 'It'll only be until I finish my shift?'

'Of course, I'll look out some of Maggie's things to take up tomorrow. I can't believe she's on the mend. Was she awake while you were there?' Bernice looped her arm through Stacey's.

'Erh, Bernice,' Nick interrupted. 'We haven't finished our chat?'

'We can chat anytime. We girls have work to do, and judging by the noise out in the bar so do you two.'

Stacey fell asleep not long after they arrived at Maggie's house. Wredd wasn't home. Bernice chose some pyjamas and toiletries to take to Maggie in the hospital next day. She spotted a couple of library books by Maggie's bed so she popped those into the bag, too.

There were two tumblers in the kitchen, sitting by a half empty bottle of brandy. Bernice pushed open the patio doors and was about to empty an overflowing ashtray into the bin when a thought came into her head. MacIntosh had been here. These were his cigar butts. Those two had been here enjoying themselves in Maggie's home while she was lying up in the infirmary. Bernice ground her teeth. She gently lifted each glass with the protection of kitchen roll, stretched cling film over the ashtray and slipped the debris into a carrier bag. Then she went into the bathroom to look for Wredd's razor. Sure enough, there it sat, with his stubble impregnated on a soapy puddle nearby. More than enough, she thought as she locked the front door.

Bernice slipped the key through the letterbox and headed home with a cacophony of spells swirling in her mind.

Chapter 22

Back at the farm, Dermott twitched. 'Maybe you should do this on your own.'

Mrs McEwan handed him a bundle of letters. 'No, we both need to sort this out. I'll tell you everything.'

'Why me though, surely Mr McEwan is better to help with this?'

'Oh, Mr McEwan already knows the truth, as does that drunken father of yours. It won't go away. Not now that Bernice is stirring it all up.'

Dermott rubbed his aching head. 'I don't understand. Stirring what up?'

'Look, Tam McShane, your excuse for a father, has admitted he took advantage of Bernice, and because of him she left the island.'

'She could have stayed, sure, her mother stayed when she was having her.'

'That was different. Bernice's mother was a troubled soul after her man left with the caravans. She was young, in love, besotted even.'

'He never came back for her. The traveller, he never came back.' Dermott looked bemused.

'Oh but he did. That's the point. Bernice's father did come back. Sure, he never knew when he left that her mother was carrying his child, but all credit to him, he did come back for Bernice's mother.'

Dermott scratched his scalp and winced.

'O'Hanlon and your old man met up with the travellers. They tracked them down on one of the other islands. They warned them off from coming back here.' Mrs McEwan settled her back against the pillows.

'Why would they do that? Wouldn't O'Hanlon want his

daughter wed?'

'Married to a traveller?' Mrs McEwan shook her head. 'O'Hanlon felt emancipated. He liked to be in control. His pride crashed when the pregnancy became noticeable. The shame weighed heavily on his shoulders.'

'Surely the traveller would have been a help on the farm?'

'It would have been another mouth to feed, and what with a baby, too? No. O'Hanlon said the travellers bred like rabbits. He worried this one would outshine him. Never took it well that he had no son of his own.' Mrs McEwan dabbed at her eyes. 'Not enough to have a beautiful daughter and grand-daughter. Jeez, I would have cherished them both.'

'He took me and Robbie in, when things got too bad with our old man.'

'I know he did, Dermott. As unpaid labourers, it was never any more than that.'

Dermott's jaw dropped.

Mrs McEwan soothed him. 'Perhaps in his own way he loved you like sons, if that man ever knew how to love.'

Dermott looked away as Mrs McEwan dabbed at her eyes again.

'So, Bernice's mother, did she know her man tried to come back?'

'Not at first. Not for a long time. He wrote to her.' She pointed at the pink dance bag. 'Granny O'Hanlon was sick with worry. Torn between telling her daughter and losing both her and her only grandchild, for no way would the traveller be allowed back here to settle as family. He did come back though. In the depth of the night he came on a fishing boat and took Bernice's mother away with him.'

'Bernice's mother drowned?'

'No. Some of us knew the truth. We wanted to spare Bernice. It seemed the best thing to do.'

'Where is she now then, Bernice's mother? Why didn't they

take the baby with them?' Dermott's voice sounded uncharacteristically forceful.

'In time, in time you will find out. We need to stop Bernice from digging. No good can come of it.'

'I don't understand. Liam? Where does Liam fit into all of this?'

'What do you mean?'

'You said O'Hanlon never had a son. He went to his grave with the bitterness.'

'Liam was the spoils of a wicked gamble.'

Dermott shook with rage.

'What are you on about you daft 'aul bat? You saying Liam was put up as collateral for some poker game?'

Mrs McEwan began to cry. Her whole body shook as the tears fell freely.

'Well!' Dermott raised his voice again. 'What rubbish are you telling me?'

'You need to understand. We're talking years ago. The island wasn't as it is now. People, traditions, everything was different, so very different.'

'Was it so different that, you traded in human traffic?'

'It wasn't like that Dermott. Oh please try and understand.'

Dermott paced the floor. His breathing was loud and fast. Suddenly his arm shot out in front of him as he punched the wall. Mrs McEwan clasped her hands over her face and wept uncontrollably.

The pain in his fist didn't deflect his anger the way he had hoped. Dermott leant his forehead against the wall and tried to steady his breathing. Finally, he turned to face Mrs McEwan. Dermott crouched before her and laid his head in her lap, like he had done as a child. Mrs McEwan stroked his hair and sniffed.

'I am so sorry! Things got out of hand. We were all trying our best,' she said.

Dermott looked up at her.' Best to do what, to separate

families, to destroy lives, to cause pain and suffering?'

'Sit with me, Dermott. Let's sort through the letters. Maybe then you'll understand.'

Dermott sat on the bed but didn't lift any letters.

'What's to understand? What could possibly make this situation understandable? My whole life has been a lie. Robbie's the fortunate one. He'll never have to try and get his head around this shambles.'

'Let's sort in date order first. Then we can read them together.' Mrs McEwan forced a small bundle of letters into Dermott's hand, knowing his literary skills were pretty poor.

Chapter 23

Wredd sat across from MacIntosh and watched him take long, slow drags at a stubby cigar.

'Women find this real sexy,' the older man shared. 'Havana. The smell of money, success, power.'

'Take it you had no cigars the night Bernice went back to yours after Maggie's leaving do at the salon?'

MacIntosh spluttered. 'Don't mock me, Wredd. At least I got her back to my place. You've been sniffing around Bernice for years.'

'How did you get off the balcony?'

'The thing is, after a night of rampant love making, one enjoys a snooze under the stars. Bernice wanted to leave early that's all. Think I exhausted her. The wind must have closed the door over. My cleaner released me when she started her shift the next day.'

'Bernice tells it differently. She and Maggie thought it all hilarious, you lying out there in your birthday suit.'

MacIntosh threw the cigar to the ground and stubbed it with his shoe.

'Aw come on, Mac. That's why we make such a good team. You're the brains, and I'm the brawn.' Wredd preened.

Macintosh puffed out his chest and sucked in his belly. 'Without me you're nothing, Wredd – a broken down sportsman with a passion for killing.'

'Killing? It's called slaughtering and that's what cattle are bred for.'

'And you? What are you bred for? Look at yourself. You're a nobody with no past and a future that depends on me.'

'How do you work that out? You need me to do your dirty work.'

'My dirty work? You been watching those old Cagney movies again? The dirtiest you've ever got from working for me was when your fountain pen burst when you were signing off the hotel bill in Dubai.' Macintosh took a sheaf of papers from his desk drawer. He perched reading glasses on his nose and flicked through the documents.

'Tell me what we going to do now then?' Wredd asked.

MacIntosh ignored him.

'What now, Mac, have I to beg for instructions like a dog for a bone? You said this was a partnership.'

MacIntosh removed the spectacles and let them dangle from his hand. He looked directly at Wredd. 'The new spa is launching soon. There is work to be done but if you're determined to prance around drawing attention to yourself, maybe it's time I let you go.'

'Let me go! I don't think so. I know too much. You promised me all the bread I could dream of. All I've had so far is a few crumbs. You need to wise up. It's not me that's the liability. You're losing it.'

'I think not. Look, we're both feeling the pressure. I'm more used to it than you. You need to slow down. Stash your cash. Buy a bread bin on expenses for the dough. Don't invite awkward questions.'

'So far as anyone knows, I've been working abroad, making big bucks.'

'Maggie? If she files for divorce, don't you think her lawyers will delve into your accounts? Check your source of earnings? Have you thought of how you'll explain that?'

'Maggie won't divorce me. She couldn't cope without this old love machine. It's Bernice filling her head with ideas. We need to get shot of Bernice.'

'How exactly, press an electrode to her head and serve her up as hamburger?'

'No. It's much simpler. Bernice has a family drama going on and has come into some property, and it's tucked away in a far flung corner of the Highlands. Don't know the full details but that Liam, he knows. I'll get it out of him, too. I'm sure if I make an attractive enough offer we can get shot of both of them back to Banjoville.'

The telephone rang. MacIntosh picked it up, covered the handset with his hand and mouthed, 'Later. We'll speak later.'

Wredd took his cue and left the room.

The high street was fairly busy. Wredd leaned against a wall and lit a cigarette. He looked up at Bernice's flat.

Behind the curtains, Bernice laughed gently over a glass of red wine, secure in the knowledge that her recent spell would have broken up the bromance between Wredd and MacIntosh.

Across the road, another man sat in the window of a coffee shop watching Wredd with interest. A waitress laid a fresh drink on the man's table. The mug nudged a newspaper and spilled a little of the coffee.

'Oh I'm so sorry. Is it all right?' she asked.

The man lifted a small Dictaphone from under the newspaper and gave it a quick rub with his sleeve. 'No harm done.'

'Are you sure everything's all right?' the waitress asked as she dabbed at the soggy mess with a cloth.

'It will be,' he murmured. 'Everything will be all right now.'

Chapter 24

Maggie was due home from hospital. Her house smelled of carpet freshener and bleach. Stacey plumped up cushions and laid them out symmetrically, while Bernice followed and bundled the cushions into heaps of abstract colour.

'I've got macaroni, the good stuff, from "Papa Joey's". They don't normally do takeaway.'

'Maybe she'll want something a bit easier on the digestion.'

Stacey stood very still, as though mulling over the suggestion. 'Macaroni's her favourite.'

'I can't argue with that.' Bernice smiled 'She hasn't said much has she?'

'Don't suppose there's much to say when you're stuck in a hospital bed for weeks.'

The two reached simultaneously for a large pillow on Maggie's bedroom floor. They bumped heads and laughed.

Stacey held the pillow close to her body as she lay back on the bed. Bernice lay beside her. For a few moments they laughed and focussed on the ceiling. Then they studied the cornicing for a while.

'Mum is okay, Bernice, isn't she?'

'They wouldn't send her home if she wasn't on the mend.'

'How could she catch a virus that knocked her out like that?'

'Who knows? Who cares? If nothing else it's given your mum time to rest. Hopefully that'll be an end to the headaches, too.'

'Dad says he'll pick her up. He's borrowing MacIntosh's car.'

Bernice thought back to her own journey in that car and the smugness of its driver.

'Strange how your dad's hooked up with him, don't you think?'

'Why so strange?'

'Well, he sacked me, reported me to Inland Revenue and then

made your mum redundant.'

'Just business, Dad said. Maybe him giving Dad a job is MacIntosh's way of apologising?'

'I heard he's opening up a flash new place, and he hasn't asked your mum or me to go work for him. Not that either of us would.'

Stacey stretched her legs.

'Your mum was loyal to him for years, Stacey. The redundancy package didn't last long, especially with Wredd moving away so suddenly.'

Stacey stood. 'Dad's back now. He earned loads working away. Mum won't need to work at all, stop being so negative.'

Bernice sat upright on the bed. 'I'm being realistic. You do know that your mum doesn't want to be with him anymore. Nothing's changed.'

Stacey dropped the pillow. 'You don't know that for sure, Mum and Dad will be fine.' She left the room.

Bernice sat dangling her legs over the end of the bed. She reached down to retrieve the pillow. The valance was tucked awkwardly under the mattress, hanging like a row of condemned buildings.

Bernice knelt on the floor and lifted the mattress slightly to straighten the pleats. It was then that she first saw the package.

Chapter 25

The island was cloaked in humidity and Robbie was feeling tired and light-headed. He didn't need Dermott making all the decisions for him, he thought. He worked hard, man's work. He deserved a man's reward.

Wandering into Clancy's bar, he ordered a pint and a shot of whiskey.

'Well, well, Son.' McShane rested his arm on Robbie's shoulder. 'Finally manning up are we?'

Robbie took the beer and downed it in one. He hiccupped.

McShane laughed and slapped him on the back. 'It gets easier with time. Everything does.'

Robbie knocked back the shot of whiskey in one quick motion. His face paled and he gagged.

'Same again barman,' McShane ordered.

They drank all afternoon like duelling banjos.

At the farm, Dermott wandered outside. 'Robbie!' he called.

He checked the barn, the shed and looked across the fields. There was no sign of his younger brother. Going back inside, he went into Robbie's bedroom. The unmade bed and pile of rotting socks may have been enough to keep some folks at bay but Dermott had taken a deep breath before entering. He nudged the foot of the bed and poked around the sheets – no sign of life. He kicked a few odd socks out onto the landing and picked up a magazine from the carpet. The adventures of Spiderman had always been a favourite of Robbie's and the magazine was well worn. As Dermott flicked through the pages, a smaller publication fell to the floor. Dermott picked it up. 'Well, well, wee brother. It looks like Wonder Woman may take old Spider's place in your heart.' Dermott turned the smaller magazine one way then the other and smiled. 'The boy's all grown up.'

Dermott headed down to Clancy's bar.

Robbie's head was hanging to one side as he listened with feigned interest as McShane gabbled on.

'So I say to him...'

'Robbie?' Dermott went straight to his brother. 'Have you been drinking?'

'Sho whats if I has?' Robbie slurred.

Dermott turned to McShane. 'This is down to you, I take it?' he asked as Robbie toppled against his shoulder.

'Notsh feelin so great.' Robbie tried to stand, his weight heavy against his brother.

Dermot slung Robbie's arm over his shoulder and half carried him towards the gents toilet. Robbie's feet dragged across the floor leaving a track of muddy skid marks.

A few moments later, Dermott emerged alone. McShane sat with his back to the toilets. Dermott swung the older man around on his bar stool.

'He's in there chucking his guts up.' Dermott's face tightened.

'At least he's got guts,' McShane replied.

'I would never cease to enjoy smashing your face off a pavement.'

'Love you too, Son.'

Dermott grabbed McShane by the throat. He stared into his father's bloodshot eyes.

'Come on now,' the barman said, 'the boy ordered the first round.'

'Indeed,' replied McShane. 'Nothing beats spending time with family, especially in such a pleasant establishment.'

Dermott tightened his grip. 'Why don't you just die?' He let McShane go.

McShane straightened up and pulled a dirty handkerchief from his jacket. He covered his mouth with the cotton, coughed loudly and spat into the hanky.

'There's a young pup in there spewing his liver up,' a customer said as he reached the bar.

'What's it to you?' Dermott clenched his fists.

'Nothing to me, friend. I'm thinking maybe he needs a hand right now, bleating like a lamb back there.'

Dermott left to find Robbie. The barman served the customer and went back to cleaning glasses. McShane looked towards the gents and then back at his beer. He chose to focus his attention on the drink and didn't see Dermott help Robbie out into the car park. But someone did. The man flicked a cigarette butt to the ground and watched the brothers stagger off into the distance. Then he headed for the ferry terminal.

To wait.

Chapter 26

Bernice was on her way back to the island. She walked the length of the deck on the ferry, looking around for the steward from her previous journey, back to Glasgow, when Maggie was in hospital. Had she imagined that tattoo on his forearm? "Always Hope". The Tarot card she'd found on the counter, the Wheel of Fortune, was in her hand. What, she asked herself, was she hoping to achieve from this latest visit to her childhood home? Bernice watched the island grow from a dot in the distance to a jewel of greenery as the ferry docked. It was a dull day with rain clouds overhead. The island was shrouded in a fine mist as she disembarked.

'Magical isn't it?' The man appeared at her side.

Bernice turned at the sound of his voice. 'Indeed.'

His face was half hidden by a scarf looped around his neck.

'Do I know you?' Bernice asked.

'Does anyone really know anyone?' He touched her arm. She flinched and he let his hand drop.

'Unusual scarf you have there. Hand knitted?' she asked.

'Fisherman's rib. The pattern.' He loosened the scarf letting it hang from his shoulders like a priest's stole.

Bernice reached out and felt the thickness of the wool. 'Hebridean Aran.'

'May I walk with you?' he asked.

Bernice faltered. 'Weren't you waiting for the ferry?' She looked in his eyes for signs of madness.

'I was waiting for you.'

Bernice took a step back.

'You won't remember me,' he continued.

Bernice picked up on his accent. The lilt of his voice was surely the melody of a travelling man.

'I don't know you.'

'Bernadette.' He held her gaze. 'I'm your father.'

They must have walked together to the farm. Bernice wiped her brow several times along the way, finally taking off her coat as her temperature continued to rise. She took slow purposeful strides, holding the coat close. The man carried her holdall.

Bernice stopped at the front door of the farmhouse and once more reached for his scarf. 'Granny?'

'She always had a soft spot for me, your granny did.' He smiled.

Bernice felt a little light-headed. As he removed his cap, she saw sprigs of copper curls spring up and tumble over his ears. He pulled a leather wallet from his jacket and opened it to show a faded photo booth image.

'Mum?' Bernice rubbed her thumb across the plastic pocket. 'I don't have any photos. Grandad, well, he didn't talk about her much. The only images I have are the faded ones I have in my head.'

'Shall we go in?' He pushed the door.

Half-empty dishes sat on the table, newspapers were strewn across the hearth. It was obvious to Bernice that Dermott and Robbie had taken advantage of her absence and moved back in.

'I must be off my head.' Her voice sounded higher pitched than usual. 'You're a stranger to me and yet here I am inviting you into my home.'

'It's not your home, though is it?' He started to clear the table. 'I'm not a stranger either.'

Bernice stared at him.

'I don't think this here farm holds happy memories for either of us. Do you?'

Bernice smoothed down her skirt, picked at the multi coloured beading and chewed at the end of her hair.

The man laughed. 'You are so like your mother. She would have been proud to bits of you.'

'How do you know? If what you say is true, you abandoned us.'

The man sat by the fire and looked up at his daughter. 'Is that what they told you?'

'It's what I know. Mum fell into some sort of depression and ended up walking into the sea.'

'In the name...' He stooped forwards and rested his head on his hands. When he looked up Bernice could see tears on his cheeks. 'Your mother didn't drown. I came back for her. Granny was supposed to bring you to the boat but she never showed up. We weren't sure if your grandad had discovered our plan, but we couldn't take any chances. With daylight almost upon us, we had to leave. Your mother and me, we had to get away from this toxic island.'

'You left me here, though, is that what you are saying?'

'We wrote to you. All of the time.'

'Who did?'

'Your mother and me, we never stopped trying to bring you back to us. Is there anything to drink around here?' he asked.

Bernice pulled a bottle of whiskey from the sideboard and poured a large tumbler full. She handed it to her newly acquired father.

'I won't,' she said. 'Need a clear head to take all of this in.'

The spluttering of an old truck outside startled them both. Standing in the breeze from the doorway was a breathless Mrs McEwan. She laid the pink dance case on the table.

'The blacksmith said he saw you coming up here.'

'So what if he did?' Bernice asked. 'You know who this is?'

Mrs McEwan heaved herself into an armchair.

'Sure, 'tis your faither,' she wheezed.

Bernice stared at her for a few seconds. The man lifted the whiskey bottle and offered it to Bernice. She pushed a tumbler towards him and accepted the measure he poured. The drink stung her tongue. That didn't stop her asking for more. She ignored the burning in her throat.

'Okay. Let's get this reunion started. Who's going to tell me what's going on?'

Chapter 27

The pink vanity case sat on one side of the table, the biscuit tin on the other. Mrs McEwan emptied the contents onto the scored wood. Bernice lifted a few of the envelopes and laughed.

'Letters tied with ribbon, really? What decade is this?'

Mrs McEwan shifted in her chair. 'We did what we thought was best.'

'Who thought it was best? Who was it best for?'

Bernice's father rested his hand over hers. 'We are where we are. Let's see if we can make any sense of this before any more hearts get broken.'

'The voices of reason are you?' Bernice fanned the envelopes across the table's worn surface. 'My whole life I've felt shame and guilt. You think a few scraps of paper are going to make up for that?'

'It might help bring closure. Peace,' her father suggested. 'I felt the same as you for years and it near destroyed me. Please. Let's work together to make sense of it all? Spend time together? No more lies? No more secrets?'

Bernice clawed at her hair. 'I want to feel something. Not anger. Not rage. I want my life to have meant something!'

'You were always loved,' Mrs McEwan interrupted.

'So much so that Granny lied? Let me go it alone in a strange city with no family? Let me think my crazed mother had drowned when all the time she was living over the brush with her fancy man. I can just imagine her packing for that trip. Let's see, toothbrush, check, hairdryer, check, daughter...oh, probably don't need her.'

'Maybe we should get Dr Manson to come over? Give you something to calm you?' Mrs McEwan offered.

'Maybe you should both leave now. Leave and let me clear my head. I know where to find you, if I want to.'

Bernice's father helped Mrs McEwan to the door. The older woman rushed outside into the arms of her waiting husband. Bernice's father stood on the step and looked back at her. She waved him to leave. Once the noise from the truck faded away, Bernice threw herself onto the floor, her melancholy heightened by the whiskey.

She lay face down like a weeping star.

Chapter 28

Back in Glasgow Nick was pleased to get the call. He found it difficult to hear what Bernice was saying through her sobs but at least she was in touch.

'Need you here, Nick. I have so much to tell you. I don't know where to turn.'

* * *

Being the owner of a bar had its advantages.

'I'll be gone a few days,' Nick called to his staff. 'You take instructions from Elizabeth, Liam.'

Stacey relaxed on a barstool. 'Is everything okay with Bernice? It's just we haven't heard from her.'

'Sure. She just wants a hand with moving some stuff,' Nick lied. 'Probably needs a hunk of beefcake to scare that Dermott and Robbie away.' He raised his arms like a body builder.

Stacey squeezed one of Nick's biceps.

'Mmm, size of a frozen pea. That Dermott could blow you away like a dandelion.'

'Dandelion's have their uses. Not only can you tell the time with them, they make a great white wine and you can shred the leaves into a salad.'

Stacey smiled. 'They make you pee the bed! Away you go! You are such a weed, Nick, just like a dandelion.'

'Who says dandelions are weeds? I like to think of them as miniature sunflowers.' Nick smiled.

* * *

Once Nick was gone, Liam and Stacey took time out in the back room of the bar.

'You sure Bernice is okay?' Liam asked.

'She's a scatterbrain at times, but I'm sure she'll get everything sorted. She's not really spoken to you though?'

'Not *really* spoken, no. It's too strange. Not sure whether I'm her brother, her uncle or just something the auld man defrosted one night when Ma was at bingo.'

'Never knew she gambled.'

'She didn't. You've no idea how it feels to be caught up in all of this. Wish we could just disappear. Go abroad and leave them all to sort out the mess.' Liam moved magazines to the floor. 'Stacey, we don't really know each other so well. Heck, I don't even know myself, but I want us to be together.'

'We are together.'

'We're in your parent's house. With your mum still not 100 per cent. It's not ideal is it?'

'Mum can't help being ill, Liam.'

'I know. It's your da's place to look out for her though? We're young. Free. Let's just pack up and go.'

'I can't leave my mum. Not right now.'

'I don't think I can stay around your da. He treats me like a wasp in his underpants.'

'I'm his little girl. He's just being protective.'

'He's a wannabe gangster, Stacey.'

'You're tired, Liam. I get that. Dad's no gangster. That's ridiculous.'

'What about MacIntosh? Bad news, so he is. Your da follows him like a rent boy follows a sugar daddy.'

Stacey kicked the magazines that were lying on the floor. 'That's enough! At least I know who my family are! Maybe you're jealous!' She stormed out of the building.

Liam followed but only got as far as the bar.

'Erh, getting busy, Son, you need to step up, especially with Nick being away.' Wredd stood beside MacIntosh grinning. 'Trouble in paradise or has my Stacey come to her senses and dumped you? Two large brandies.'

Liam served the drinks. His left eyelid twitched.

'So, Nick is headed back to the island I hear. That Bernice reels him in like a fish.' Wredd spoke to no one in particular.

Liam headed to the gents toilet. He sat in a cubicle with his feet against the door. Taking a deep breath, he thought how Granny would have dealt with all of this. But what was all of this? Who were his parents? Why all the secrets?

'Oh bus boy!' Wredd called through the door. 'If you're too busy in there feeling sorry for yourself, I'll just help myself to another drink shall I?'

Liam kicked the door, unbolted it and stood at the washbasin. He looked at his reflection in the mirror as he let cold water run over his wrists.

Wredd was soon behind the bar juggling bottles of spirits and squirting long shots into tall glasses. A small crowd gathered eager to accept the free drinks.

'Enough!' Elizabeth, the barmaid came through from the kitchen. 'Get back to your side of the bar and stop giving the boy a hard time!'

Wredd grabbed a bottle of brandy and shunted back to stand with MacIntosh.

'I'll have that back 'an all.' Elizabeth reached across for the bottle. She threw a cold glance at the dispersing crowd. 'Or thirty quid should cover it.' She held her hand out towards Wredd.

'I'll happily pay double.' MacIntosh laughed. 'The entertainment value alone is worth more.' He handed over a few banknotes.

'Now sit down and shut up, or drink up and get out.' Elizabeth had worked too many years in bars to take any nonsense from the punters.

Wredd and MacIntosh moved to a booth where they spent the next few hours in huddled conversation.

Liam phoned Stacey several times, until her voicemail refused to record anymore.

Chapter 29

A night's sleep worked better than any medicine Dr Manson could prescribe. Bernice showered and dressed, lightly poached a couple of eggs and waited for Nick to arrive. He did so just after nine, with a rucksack on his back and a pet carrier in his hand.

'Great, you caught the early ferry?' Bernice smiled. 'Oh and you've brought Hex.' Bernice rushed to free the cat. Hex leapt onto the floor and proceeded to take a tour of the farmhouse and mark his new territory.

'Course I did. You sounded really down. You're looking good now though.'

'I met my father yesterday.' Bernice buttered fresh toast.

'Your father? I thought he disappeared before you were born?'

'He's re-appeared now, and apparently, how about this, Nick, my mother never drowned.'

Nick's opened his eyes wide along with his silent mouth.

'Dear Mommy eloped with dear Daddy but forgot to take little old me,' Bernice spoke in an exaggerated childish whine.

'That can't be right.' Nick chewed on a crust.

'I would say it's not right but according to my old man, with Mrs McEwan backing him up, there we have it. It wasn't *he* who abandoned *us*. It was *them* who abandoned *me*.'

'No, that's obscene. Your granny would've known. She would've told you the truth?'

'Oh Granny knew. It seems like quite a few folk around here knew, just not me. More tea?'

'Where's this father of yours been all this time? Why has he re-appeared now? Where's your mother? Why's she not with him?'

'That, my dear Nick, is what we're going to find out. That and a whole lot more about my mysterious family. They've left a pile of letters and documents for me to go through.'

A trio of familiar figures cast a shadow in the doorway.

'Ah, Dermott, I wondered when you would show up.' Bernice poured tea into a fresh cup.

'I heard you were back. Sorry about the mess.' Dermott wore his work clothes, cap in hand.

'Come in please, come in,' Bernice said cheerfully. 'Mess, you're apologising for the mess? You mean the leftover chicken wings or my life?'

Nick chewed the toast to mush.

Dermott stepped aside as Mrs McEwan and Bernice's father crowded into the small room. They sat at the big table whilst Dermott took up residence in the armchair by the fire. Bernice dipped into the pink vanity case and slid a letter from an envelope. She held the paper in her hand and looked at the man who claimed to be her father.

'Where's my mother then? Too scared to face me herself?'

He cupped his hands and blew into them a couple of times.

'She's gone. That's partly why I wanted to find you again. I need to close the circle.'

'Are you looking for sympathy, telling me about your loss?' Bernice pushed her hair back before pinning it high on her head like a crown. She secured it with a jewelled clip.

'I've just buried my granny. Grandad was no great loss to me. I've had to face the man who took advantage of me all those years ago and have been presented with a teenage lad from who knows where, claiming to be my relation. Now you show up looking to play happy families. Tell you what, mister, that pack of cards has a few missing.'

'I've been looking for you, following you, trying to find the right time to approach you.'

'Have you really? For how long have you been stalking me?'

'Not stalking. Trying to see what kind of a life you've had, when best to tell you about what happened. To fill in the gaps'

'Fill in the gaps? It's taken you over twenty years to pluck up the courage? Go grow a pair!'

Mrs McEwan broke into the conversation.

'No point arguing about the past. We're where we are. Read the letters. Maybe that'll help.'

Bernice scanned the letter in her hand then pushed it towards the man.

'Sentimental rubbish, poor you, how much you must have missed me, longed to be with me. Load of nonsense. You knew where I was. You never came back for me.'

Mrs McEwan started to cry.

'Forget the crocodile tears. You had no right to keep these letters from me. They may be clichéd drivel but they were for me. Not you. Who do you think you are, interfering in other folk's lives like this?'

'You were a child. Your grandad was manipulative. I was scared of what he'd do if he found out that your parents were trying to keep in touch.'

'Scared? Did Granny know about the letters?'

The room was silent.

'I asked you a question?'

'Yes.' Mrs McEwan trembled as she spoke.

'Oh, forget the dramatics. So Granny knew? Why didn't she take me to my parents? If not the first time, at the boat, why not later? She could have stayed there too?' Bernice stood quickly and paced the room.

'Our lives could have been so different!' She placed her hands flat on the table and leaned close to Mrs McEwan's face. 'Did they…my parents…know what happened to me? What McShane did?'

Mrs McEwan nodded.

'We knew. I wanted to kill him, to rip his head from his shoulders,' her father raised his voice.

'Oh, is that right?' Bernice shrugged. 'What stopped you? He'll be over there, in Clancy's bar, pouring booze down the neck of that head, which, as you know, is still attached to him.'

'It wasn't straightforward,' Mrs McEwan interrupted.

Bernice turned to Nick. 'Get them out of here, before I'm the one to start ripping heads off.'

Nick laid his hand on the man's arm. 'Maybe let her sleep on it.'

'She's slept enough. It's time to wake up and face what we're trying to explain,' Bernice's father replied.

Mrs McEwan was on her feet twisting and turning the gold ring on her finger.

'Let it go, Bernice. We all make mistakes. There's no point in digging this all up again. It can only cause you more heartache.'

'What do you know about heartache? You have no idea. Absolutely no idea how hurt I've been. All these years feeling ashamed, frightened. You could have passed these letters onto me at any time. I'm not Peter Pan. I've grown up.'

Nick opened the farmhouse door and stood by it with his elbow resting on the frame.

'As for you and your fatherly advice.' Bernice turned to her father. 'I'll out-sleep Rip Van Winkle if I choose to. All these years and you expect me to let it go? I don't think so.' Bernice stood with her hands on her hips. 'Humiel is your grandson. Where is he, where is my son? If you two know so much, tell me what happened to Humiel?'

The unwelcome guests turned to leave. Bernice called after them.

'I will find the truth! You know I will.'

It was Dermott who turned in reply. 'Robbie and me, we're not responsible, you know it was the elders who made the decisions back in those days.'

'Not any more, Dermott.' Bernice's eyes glinted with determination. 'Not any more.'

Nick and Bernice sat together on the sofa.

'You didn't ask much about your mother?'

Bernice shrugged. 'Some mother she was, running off like

that. I'd never leave any child of mine to fend for theirselves.' She paused. 'They knew what happened to me, Nick. She never even came to comfort me. Now she never can, he said she's gone, dead, unless she's cowering in Mrs McEwan's back room, waiting to see my reaction.'

'Maybe they are right, in some way, maybe reading the letters would help.'

'This is not some cheap mystery magazine. I will seek help to understand in my own way, in my own time. If they would just be open about Humiel. I need to know.'

'Bernice, they wouldn't have taken your baby away. He must have died like they said. You were young, immature, maybe your body didn't cope with the birth.'

'My body coped fine. It's my mind that's struggling. You go, Nick, please, go for a walk. Give me a couple of hours?'

'If that's what you want. I'm trying to help.'

Bernice kissed him lightly on his forehead. Nick held her in his arms for a few seconds until she gently pushed him away.

'A couple of hours it is,' Nick agreed.

* * *

With Nick gone, Bernice was free to clear her mind and focus on her next step. She took her Book of Shadows and flicked through the pages. With the book in one hand, she clutched a handful of Banded Agate crystals: green aventurine – the "Stone of Heaven." The all-round healer: mental, emotional and physical, soothing, healing, and balancing. It opened and soothed a wounded heart. Bernice focussed on her breathing until she reached a state of calm. Then she lay the book down. Hex slurped noisily at a bowl of water. Bernice locked the door and pulled the curtains closed. The heavy material kept the daylight at bay. She lit candles all around the room, warmed oil in a diffuser: sweet basil to stimulate and clear the conscious mind, reduce fatigue and allow the correct path to reveal itself. The old biscuit tin from Dermott sat on the table. Various documents, certificates and trinkets lay within. Bernice lifted a worn pack of Tarot cards from the pile and shuffled through them. She counted to make sure the full deck was there. Usually she worked with an Albano Waite with a deck of 78: 26 Major Arcana and 56 Minor Arcana. The cards from the tin were more subtle in colour, more like the original Rider Waite. She split the deck into five suits. The Major Arcana: The Fool, The Magician, The High Priestess, The Empress, The Emperor, The Hierophant, The Lovers, The Chariot, Strength, The Hermit, The Wheel of Fortune, Justice, The Hanged Man, Death, Temperance, The Devil, The Tower, The Star, The Moon, The Sun, Judgment, The World and the four Minor Arcana: Pentacles, Wands, Cups, and Swords. Bernice touched each card softly and rested her hands palms down in front of her. Closing her eyes, she sat still, letting her thoughts go back to her childhood and her early introduction to the cards that were to play such an important part in later life. *Granny kept the family rosary beads by her bed and the Tarot cards hidden away. With Grandad at Clancy's bar, she took time to practice her true passion, encouraging Bernice to watch, listen and learn. Bernice remembered how serene Granny looked when she worked with the cards.* Hex jumped onto the table and curled his tail around his paws. He stared at the cards but did not disturb her concentration. Bernice had discovered meditation when she was very young. As an adult, she truly appreciated the tranquillity and clarity that it brought her, preferring to meditate outdoors. She found that the sights, sounds and smells of nature enhanced the experience. Not today. She felt the urge to re-charge and focus on how she would go forwards. The farmhouse was isolated and with so many having being asked to stay away, Bernice felt confident she would benefit from some time to herself. The events of previous months had taken their toll and she felt emotionally drained. In the peaceful surroundings that she had created, Bernice breathed slowly, consciously focussing on every breath until she felt completely in control of her mind. Her aim was to be receptive and alert. If she lay down, she feared the previous nights of broken sleep could take over. With her eyes still closed, Bernice imagined a bluebell in her mind, the flower growing from a seed, breaking through the soil, reaching for sunlight, accepting the rain. Growing from a tiny bud, its delicate petals curling into the familiar bell shape as it hung its head. *Granny had shared stories with her. Rarely did she need a book to prompt her. The old woman created magical tales of fairies and nature that brightened and inspired her granddaughter's imagination.* Bernice focused on her breath a few minutes more. With her breathing calm and steady, she concentrated her awareness on her feet and moved her focus gradually all the way up her body. The aim was to release any tension that she felt anywhere within her and to stop and focus on the tension asking why it was there. She visualized positive energy filling her being. Inhaling, she pictured white light entering her feet all the way to the top of her head. Slowly, she exhaled and released the white light, allowing it to enclose her in her magical space. She focussed on the image of the bluebell a while longer, opened her eyes and began to jot down notes in her Book of Shadows. The words flowed like water from a dam. A few hieroglyphics marked the page.

Bernice ended her meditation session by giving thanks for things she was grateful for in her life. She felt refreshed as she snuffed out the candles. Leaving the incense burning, she drew back the curtain to welcome the daylight. Hex was sleeping. The cards lay in sequence across the table. Bernice looked closer at the spread; one card was missing, The Wheel of Fortune.

She unzipped her handbag and pulled out the card from the steward on the ferry. Its worn edges matched the others.

'What do you think, Hex? A Fool or an Empress?'

Chapter 30

Maggie was at home resting, looking over the Glasgow cul-de-sac that had been her marital home and now felt like her prison. Stacey was with her, silent and sullen.

'Fancy some fresh air?' Stacey suggested.

Maggie shook her head.

'Would you prefer if we go for a walk?'

Maggie shook her head.

Stacey checked her phone. Six voice messages from Liam. She wasn't ready for another confrontation.

'Mum, you need to make more effort. The physio said. Come on, we can take it slowly, it's mild outside.'

Maggie shook her head.

Wredd skipped down the stairs.

'Good morning, my lovelies, is there any breakfast on the go?'

Maggie struggled up from the sofa and grabbed Stacey's arm.

'We're going out,' Maggie spoke softly.

'Good for you. Going out later myself. Have fun girls.'

Maggie clung to Stacey all the way to the park. It was a short walk and they were in no rush.

'Is everything okay with you and Liam?' Maggie asked.

Stacey shrugged.

'That's not an answer. I worry about you getting too involved too soon. We can ask him to leave if that's what you want?'

'Don't know. Maybe. So much has happened since we met. It's a lot to deal with.'

'I know I've been a wet rag lately. It's not the just the virus. Wredd coming back really shook me up.'

'Wredd? You mean Dad?'

'Course I do, but, Stacey I need to talk to you. Soon. Is Nick working today?'

'Nick's off on a jolly, back to the island with Bernice. Don't you remember? I did tell you.'

'Course you did. Course he is.'

'We can talk now can't we.'

'I'm feeling a bit tired, Stacey. Can we leave it a while? It's not the right time.'

The park was quiet. Maggie and Stacey sat on a bench without further conversation, content in each other's company. Both women's minds busy with their thoughts. Maggie smiled at a little girl running ahead of her mother. Her chubby legs restrained by the bulk of a nappy. The child tottered along grinning all the way. Maggie recognised that adventurous determination and realised how long it had been since she saw it in her own daughter.

'Is that your phone buzzing?' Maggie asked.

'It's nothing important.'

'How do you know?'

'Leave it, Mum. Come on, let's get you home.'

'I've been cooped up way too long. Let's just sit a while. Grab a coffee?'

Stacey took her purse from her handbag. 'Black no sugar?'

'Mocha and two sugars with whipped cream. I'm off the wagon.'

'Good for you, Mum. Life's too short to count calories.' Stacey headed for the kiosk.

Maggie checked Stacey's phone. She shook her head, tucked the phone back into the bag and watched her daughter walk towards her, unsmiling, carrying two styrofoam cups.

'I can speak to Liam if you want me to.' Maggie took a cup and laid it on the bench beside her.

'It's okay, Mum, nothing serious, just all this family stuff. Bernice won't open up to Liam. He's a lost soul.'

'I haven't been there for you. I know that, I've been too wrapped up in my own troubles.'

'Maybe Dad can get your job back? He's been working with

MacIntosh?'

'I don't need help from either of them.'

'Don't be stubborn, Mum. It would do you good to get back to work, even part time.'

'I will get back to work. Not for MacIntosh though. I'm thinking of going into business with Bernice.'

'Bernice has hardly been here recently, I suppose she could do with the help, but I think she's doing more holistic therapies than beauty treatments now.'

'Good contrast then. I'll concentrate on the outside and Bernice can work her magic on their Chakras or whatever.'

'Oh, Mum. Do you think Bernice really can work magic?'

'She believes what she believes and I believe in her. Bernice has been a good friend to me. I only wish I listened more and spent less time arguing with her.'

'What do you argue about?'

'Stuff. I've dismissed her too often for going on about her son. Now I think about it more – how frightened she must have been, how she needs answers. I can't imagine how I would've coped if you were taken from me.'

'But that was different. You and Dad were together. Bernice, well, that was tragic. Maybe better for her not to have the burden of a child. She might have resented it, you know, what with the circumstances.'

Maggie licked cream from her coffee and nodded.

'Who are we to judge? We reach a crossroads in our lives, choose a path, and later wonder how different things could have been if we had chosen another route'

'Very philosophical, Mum, what's brought this on?'

The toddler wobbled close by and stopped to wave at Maggie. Maggie smiled and waved back.

'Oh, Stacey, I want the best for you. You rushed into this relationship with Liam. Maybe that was the wrong choice.'

'Mum. We're okay, we need a bit of space that's all.'

'I'm on your side. It's not that I don't like Liam. I feel sorry for him, but that's no reason for you to settle for anything less than perfect.'

'Yes, like Dad is your Mr Perfect?' Stacey smiled.

'Perfect Dad to you maybe, but relationships are different. People change, grow apart.'

'Dad's home now, surely you can work things out?'

'I've tried. I've tried so hard. Being ill made me realise that I need challenge and excitement from life. I need time for me. I'm worth more.'

'Why now though? I know he's been hospital shy but Dad loves you.'

'Let's get home, Stacey. Please? I'm so tired.'

'Is that what you wanted to talk to me about, you and Dad? You said earlier we needed to talk?'

'We will talk about your dad. We'll talk properly. Later.'

Maggie slumped to the ground.

Chapter 31

Mrs McEwan loved her little flat above the island Post Office. She scooped sugar into a pot of potatoes and lowered the gas to simmer. Her husband shook his head.

'This will be the end of us.'

'We're near the end anyways. Best go out with a clear conscience, don't you think?'

Mr McEwan strained the potatoes, rinsed them under the tap and topped up with fresh water. He sprinkled salt on the water's surface and closed the lid. Mrs McEwan busied herself at the sink scraping carrots. He walked across and placed his hands on her shoulders. He wasn't a tall man but still loomed above the frail frame of his wife. He rested his chin on her head and together they looked out at the fields beyond.

'It's never too late to go to the police,' he offered.

The scraping of vegetables was her only response.

'Or burn the letters. Get rid of the whole lot.'

Still she scraped.

'Look at that land out there. We've spent our lives grafting, getting by, not living but existing. I say we sell up and go.'

Mrs McEwan turned abruptly. 'Go? Go where?'

'Anywhere, we could travel: Europe, Asia, America.'

She turned back to the sink and sucked her finger. Droplets of blood swirled in the basin amongst the carrots.

'Oh look what you made me do,' she scolded.

'I've never made you do anything, love. It never crossed my mind to try.' He let her rest against his chest and stroked her hair. 'We've no one to leave this place to. Doubt if we've touched any lives enough for them to mourn our passing. Let's just sell up. Enjoy what time we have left. Let's get away from this tragedy.'

Mrs McEwan sucked her bleeding finger and sat at the table. 'I could do with a strong cuppa.'

Mr McEwan cleared the sink, rescued the carrots and put the kettle on to boil.

'It all got out of hand, spiralled like smoke from a factory chimney.'

Mr McEwan laughed. 'What do you know of factories, you've rarely left this island?'

'I read.'

'You read flippant Women's' magazines that paint the world by numbers. That's not proper reading.'

'We can't all be bookworms like you. It's a wonder them encyclopaedias still have ink on them you've thumbed the pages so often.'

'Here, woman, take your tea.' He handed her a china cup and saucer. 'When I was at sea…'

'Oh, here we go with, the old Navy stories. If those foreign lands were so good why did you come back here?'

'For you, I would've travelled to the moon and back to be with you.'

Mrs McEwan swiped at him with a teacloth.

'Seriously, love, there's nothing to hold us back. You've given over the letters and such. Get them back and burn them or leave Bernice to sort it.'

'Her granny was my only true friend. Bernice said some really hurtful things to me, the little madam.'

'Look at it from her point of view. It's tragic but it's not our tragedy. You did what you thought was best. You stayed loyal. It's time to let it go. It's time for us now.'

Mrs McEwan twisted the gold band on her cut finger. 'For better for worse?'

'For better, love. We've been through the worst.'

The old couple sat quietly, contemplating their future and finishing the pot of tea.

Chapter 32

Set in a small valley on the island, Clancy's bar was a time traveller's dream, except you didn't actually have to travel back in time to enjoy the history of the place. Dermott doubted that anything but the beer kegs had been changed over the years. No two chairs matched, neither in height nor wood. The tables rested on folded beer mats or bricks, which did nothing for the aesthetic ambience of the place. Most of the regular customers were relics too, none more so than Tam McShane. Dermott walked past him and sat at a corner table to enjoy a break from the day's work and wait for Robbie.

Tam sat hunched over the dregs of a stale pint of bitter. His hair flopped greasily over a bald patch on the crown of his head.

'Not looking too healthy,' Bernice's father broke McShane's train of thought.' Let me get you a fresh one?'

McShane accepted the offer without looking up, and hungrily suggested, 'Go down well with a wee, gold chaser?'

Bernice's father nodded in agreement towards the barman. 'One for yourself.' He handed over some cash.

McShane savoured the cool, fresh liquid and smacked his lips. He spat on his hand rubbed it against his thigh and extended it to the generous stranger.

Bernice's father smiled and briefly grazed the hand with his.

'So, old timer,' he asked, 'what's the low-down on this place?'

'Clancy's bar?' McShane asked.

'Not the bar, this whole area, the island.'

'Not much to tell unless you can cope with the dark history; the screaming banshees and the witchcraft?'

'Sounds interesting.'

'Doesn't it just.' McShane raised his empty glass. 'Thirsty work so it is, this story telling.'

Bernice's father spoke to the barman. 'Keep 'em coming, long as he likes.' He threw a bundle of notes onto the bar.

McShane sat upright mentally, trying to count the cash by colour as the barman swept it into the till with a flourish.

'Let's get comfortable over here? What do you say?'

McShane almost fell from the bar stool in his rush to join his newfound friend.

Once seated, McShane's tongue unravelled like a ball of knitting wool. He talked of demons and mythical creatures, folklore and fairy tales, myths and legends. The afternoon crawled towards evening without him noticing that Bernice's father barely made a dent in his glass of beer.

'Seen some strange folks around here, how about some local gossip?' he asked a befuddled McShane. 'Rumour has it there's some mystery surrounding that old farm up the back of the hill there?'

'You mean O'Hanlon's old place?'

'O'Hanlon. Yes, that's the very man. Whatever happened to him and his family?'

McShane struggled to focus. 'Oh, he died, simple as that. He keeled over right there at his wife's funeral.'

'Died? Just like that? What caused it?'

'Lack of breathing.' McShane laughed at his own joke. Then he coughed.

'Bad chest you've got there.'

'Oh, it's the auld lungs. I'm falling apart a bit at a time. Aye, but unlike poor O'Hanlon I'm still here.'

'Shame that, at his wife's funeral and all. Think it was the grief of losing his dearly beloved.'

McShane slapped the table and howled with laughter. 'O'Hanlon was a man with neither heart nor conscience. Hard to the core he was.'

'He wasn't a family man then?'

'Oh, he had family as such, but he wasn't that keen on them.'

'Why would that be?'

'He wanted a son to carry on the name. Seems he was the youngest of 12 sons and the only one not to have a boy of his own. Near broke him that did.'

The barman arrived with fresh drinks.

'He did have a daughter though?'

'Sure did. A right bundle of trouble, flighty type. Bit of a dreamer. Tried to run away and join the circus with some clown that got her in the family way.'

Bernice's father stroked his chin. 'That right?'

'We put a stop to it at first though, me and O'Hanlon. Oh, back in the day we could rustle up a posse that would have the Lone Ranger shaking in his boots, I can tell you.'

'So, is she still at the farm, the daughter?'

McShane shook his head and waved his arms. 'Not at all, she ended up in the family way then disappeared eventually. She left her daughter at the farm. Can't say O'Hanlon was too fussed on her leaving. He was none too happy about having a grand-daughter mind. Now, if she'd abandoned a grandson that would have appeased him.'

'You said O'Hanlon's daughter disappeared?'

McShane looked around the bar. The room was a mishmash of blurry figures, none of which were looking their way. 'You want secrets? I've loads of 'em.'

'Secrets about what?'

'Stuff. Secret stuff. All is not what it seems around here.' McShane tapped the side of his nose and leaned closer to his companion. 'You're not from the law are you?'

Bernice's father shook his head.

'You from the newspapers?' McShane slurred.

'I'm interested in the history of the place. No hidden motives. Secrets you said?'

Robbie entered the bar. McShane tried to focus as the young man headed his way. Robbie continued walking across the room to join Dermott.

'See him? See that boy?' McShane tugged at Bernice's father's sleeve.' Him and his brother sat over there. Hate me they do. Those two left me to work with O'Hanlon. All part of the deal.'

'What deal?'

'My sons! They're my sons. O'Hanlon see, always got what he wanted in the end. Not man enough to father his own, so he took mine.'

'I don't understand. Why? How could he?'

'To keep the secret sure.'

'Keep the secret of his daughter's disappearance?'

'No. No, his granddaughter's secret. The poor abandoned little Bernadette, or Bernice as she's known now.' McShane's slurring was difficult to understand as his words tailed off into mumbles. He looked towards the ceiling. 'My days are numbered and I'll take it to the grave with me, if only I could win back my sons.'

'I don't understand?'

'My youngest yin, Robbie. He was at that age, you know, curious like? Picked me up from here one night and it all went mayhem after that. We skidded off road at one point. I wouldn't let him drive back. Shoved him in the back of the van. It was a long time ago.'

'What happened?'

'Her. Bernadette, Bernice, whatever she calls herself now. You should have seen her strutting around in that short skirt. No wonder the boy gave in to temptation.'

'You've lost me.'

'No. I lost my boys. I took the blame, you see? Robbie isn't the brightest but he is loyal. I took the blame. The baby, I took the blame.'

Bernice's father took a stiff swig of his drink, downing more in one mouthful than he had in the rest of the evening.

McShane continued. 'O'Hanlon said it was for the best. No one would stand up to us in those days. Not even sure Robbie understood what he'd done. Boy's curiosity took over. Natural curiosity, that's all.'

'So Robbie was the father of Bernice's child?'

'Got it in one, stranger.' McShane sat back on his chair and stared at the ceiling. 'O'Hanlon took my boys as payment to keep me quiet. Worked them hard. Left me with this.' He raised his glass.

'What happened to the baby?'

McShane gurgled in the back of his throat. 'Folk think Robbie's simple. Boy's special that's all. Gentle, like his dear mother. Don't think he even understands what he did.'

'The baby, what happened after the birth?' Bernice's father asked again.

'O'Hanlon said it was weak, scrawny, and probably had the brains of its father. He said he'd deal with it.'

'Come on, man. Did Bernice's baby survive?'

'Did any of us?' McShane slumped across the table.

Bernice's father lifted McShane's head and slapped his lolling face. The barman came hurrying over.

'Hoi, mister! Is there a problem here?'

'Not at all. I'm trying to wake him up, that's all.'

'He'll be fine.' The barman stood over Bernice's father. 'Maybe time you left?'

'I'm going. Look, sorry, I really was just trying to get him awake.'

'He's in here most days. I'd take anything he says with a big pinch of salt, mate. Particularly when he's had more than the Angel's share.'

'Oh the whiskey? Right. Right. I'll maybe call in another time. He's an interesting man.'

'That's one word for him,' the barman said. He pushed McShane back against one chair, lifted his feet onto another, folded his arms across his chest and cleared the table, leaving the drunk in burial pose. Bernice's father place a pound coin over each of McShane's closed eyes and smiled at the barman as he left.

Robbie and Dermott watched the scene from across the bar.

'Do you think we should go help him home?' Robbie asked.

Dermott finished his beer.

'I can't see any reason to. What's he ever done for us?'

Chapter 33

Stacey held Maggie's hand as they waiting for the ambulance to arrive. She wiped dribble from her mother's mouth, oblivious of the small crowd gathering to see what the commotion was. Maggie's hand lay limp in her daughter's but her eyes were bright.

'We will talk about your dad, Stacey. I promise, as soon as I get over this virus.'

Stacey stood back to let the paramedics work on her mother. The crowd gradually dispersed, embarrassed by their own curiosity. The journey to the infirmary meant nothing to Stacey. The lights, the siren, the furrowed brow of the man attaching tubes and tapes to her mother as the van sped through the city traffic. She held Maggie's hand and looked without seeing at her mother's greying face.

Wredd was sharing a joke in Nick's bar with MacIntosh when he got the call. 'Calm down, love. I'll meet you there,' he told Stacey

'Problem?' MacIntosh raised an eyebrow.

'Nothing that can't wait until after another snifter.' Wredd headed to the bar. Liam was on duty and pre-empted his order. He set two, large, cognac balloons in front of Wredd.

'Stick it on my tab.' Wredd smiled just as Liam's phone buzzed.

Liam made notes on a pad beside the cash register. 'Slow down, Stacey. I can't hear what you're saying.' Liam nodded and looked towards Wredd. His face flushed, his jaw tightened. 'Do you want me to tell your dad?'

Wredd smiled and raised his glass as he caught Liam's attention.

'Oh, he's already on his way is he? Good. Thought I saw him in the bar earlier, but right enough, no sign of him now. Keep me updated.' He paused. 'Love you, too.'

Liam and Wredd held each other's gaze for a few seconds.

'Is the young yin squaring up to you?' MacIntosh laughed.

'Not a chance. Think we're reaching a level of understanding. Look, I need to go after this drink. Maggie's checked in at the NHS Hilton again.'

'Giving you the right runaround that one.' MacIntosh smiled. 'Give Maggie my love won't you.'

Liam scrubbed at the bar top as he watched Wredd leave. He checked the rota for Nick's name. Although Nick made an appearance most days, he still put himself down for contact whenever he was out of town. Nick's name was highlighted in red, with a note to the side. "Off to the isle of sick sillies. Contact only in emergency." Liam assumed Stacey would let Nick and Bernice know what was going on with Maggie. He turned his attention back to the bar.

He wished Stacey would go away with him and leave all of them behind.

Chapter 34

Nick returned from his inflicted walk around the island's green acres to find Bernice asleep on the sofa. He laid a blanket over her and gently pulled a Tarot card from her clenched fist. Placing the card on the table with the others, he resisted the urge to stack the pack neatly back into its velvet shroud. The biscuit tin and paperwork were scattered in what looked to Nick like random piles across the floor. He stepped over each bundle and settled on the armchair.

Bernice looked resplendent in her casual pose. The softness of the lilac blanket complimented her pale skin. Her hair settled like vibrant flames all around her reminded Nick of a Pre-Raphaelite painting he once saw in a gallery: Mary Magdalene by Anthony Frederick Augustus Sandys. Nick never forgot the painting nor the memory of that day spent with Bernice. He watched her sleep thinking how this was the first time he'd actually appreciated how beautiful her features were. Not perfect, but then, who was? Bernice radiated a charismatic charm that went deeper than the surface of her skin.

Nick mulled over the years since they first met. It was a given that he and Bernice were free spirits, unburdened by either family ties or the need to create any. Hence tying the knot of marriage was never an option. Instead they embraced their friendship which gradually developed into a carnal knowledge that knew the boundaries of their relationship. Looking at her now, Nick felt only loss. The loss of time spent hiding behind their emotional barriers, with each of them reassuring the other that they were strong enough to fly solo through life.

He looked around the farmhouse, at a part of Bernice's history he knew nothing about. She stirred and turned to face the back of the sofa.

Chapter 34

Nick's tears felt warm on his face as he joined Bernice in slumber.

Chapter 35

The nap did them both good. Bernice woke first. She pushed Nick's shoulder.

'Wakey-wakey.'

'Oh.' Nick swung his feet to the floor. 'What time is it?'

Hex let out a loud miaeeow.

'It's dinner time. Hex just told me.' Bernice smiled. She went off towards the kitchen with Hex trailing behind.

Nick rubbed his eyes and yawned. 'Need a hand back there?' he called.

'Nope, I'm done.' Bernice handed him a mug of tea, set a plate of cookies down and settled on the sofa. 'That's Hex happy for a while. What do you think about all of this?'

Nick glanced around at the messy room. 'I'll help you tidy.' He drank his tea.

'Not this. I mean, THIS! This whole situation. '

'Honestly?' Nick asked.

'No point in not being honest.'

Nick hesitated. 'It's pretty bizarre, you know, like secrets and lies and folk appearing and disappearing all over the place. Bizarre.'

'Life's different in the city.' Bernice sipped her tea.

'Sure is. This here though, it's like going back in time, like the folks haven't caught up with reality.'

'Oh, the reality is here Nick. Maybe in a different form but believe me it's here.' She offered him a biscuit.

'Home made?'

'I smuggled them over from the "real world".'

'I wasn't meaning to be arrogant, Bernice. I've never been to a place like this, not even passing through. It's all a bit strange for me.'

'In what way do you find it strange?'

'In the way that I don't understand it, I don't know what the big deal was about your mother having you or you having...'

'Humiel. You can say his name.'

Nick sighed. 'Maybe Maggie would be better to talk to about this.'

'Because it's women's stuff?'

'No. I just mean, well with her being a mother herself.'

'How would you deal with it, Nick, if you were a father?'

'I'm not sure I can even begin to imagine how I'd feel if I lost a child.'

'So you think the loss is less because Humiel was a newborn? For argument sake, less than if he was a toddler or a teenager?'

'No. I'm just saying, I can't empathise with you. I don't have any children.'

'What if you did?'

'That's never going to happen. Not now.'

'Maggie. Have you heard from her since you came back here?'

'No word from her or Stacey. I take it that means all is going well.'

'Hopefully all's going well. Maggie relies on you a lot, don't you think?'

'We're friends. That's it.'

'Hasn't always been just friendship though.'

'We've been through this, Bernice. Maggie and I were a long time ago. We've both moved on. In fact I was thinking, hoping, that maybe, once all of this is cleared up, maybe you and I could look at our relationship a bit closer?'

Bernice dunked a biscuit in her tea. Nick mirrored her action. 'Bernice?'

'Look, Nick. I haven't known this for long, but now that I do, and with Maggie needing extra support right now, I feel I need to tell you.'

'Tell me?'

'Oh, there's no subtle way to break this. Wredd. He isn't

119

Stacey's father.' She paused. 'You are.'

Nick's face paled.

'Nick? Did you hear me?'

'What the hell!' Nick dropped the mug. It spilled onto the floor in a gooey mess with the broken biscuit half dissolved. He stood.

'Leave it.' Bernice grabbed the sleeve of his jacket.' Did you have any clue?'

'Clue? No.' Nick slumped onto the chair. 'Maybe, years ago, I thought there might be a chance, but she married Wredd. Why would she do that?'

'She was young. You were out of the country. She was scared.'

'I was dealing with my own family, if you recall. Does Wredd know?'

'No. He's too thick to work out the maths.'

'I'm taking it Stacey doesn't know.'

'Of course she doesn't. It's not up to us to tell her neither.'

'Stacey. Jeez, all this time. I can't understand why Maggie never told me.'

'I know it's difficult to get your head around. It's reality though, just like here on the island. Not always predictable. Not always pretty. I'll wipe up this mess.'

When Bernice returned with a damp cloth, Nick was gone.

Chapter 36

Mrs McEwan was stacking shelves when Nick arrived at the shop.

'Be with you in a minute,' she called as the door opened with a chirpy chime of the bell.

Nick browsed the shelves; not a huge stock, but enough mainstays to get by until the islanders stocked up from the mainland.

'Oh. I didn't expect to see you here.' Mrs McEwan wiped her hands on her overalls.

Nick spread his hands at shoulder level. 'No worries, I'm not here to cause any stress. Just wondering, with the signal being poor, have you heard from Maggie or Stacey this last couple of days?'

'No. Any reason I should have?'

'No reason at all. Look, this character claiming to be Bernice's father, can you explain what all that's about?'

'He is her father.'

'What about her mother? Why didn't she ever face up to Bernice?'

The doorbell chimed again as a shadow cussed the floor. 'Bernice's mother is in a sanatorium.' Bernice's father stood behind Nick.

Nick turned. 'Her mother's in an asylum?'

'It's more of a hospice, where she's being looked after.'

'Hospice? You said she was gone. Bernice thinks her mother's dead, for real this time.' Nick paced the shop floor. 'You're unhinged, all of you. What's with the constant lying?'

'Isn't that obvious? Bernice's mother is very ill, her nerves are fragile. She's being cared for physically, emotionally and most importantly, spiritually. We can't allow anything to disturb her equilibrium.'

'Don't you think Bernice has the right to know that? After all this time with your crazy secrets, can't you even give her what little time may be left with her mother? What is wrong with you people?'

'All in good time, all in good time.'

Mrs McEwan ushered the two men into the back shop. The three sat around the dining table.

Nick coughed. 'I'm really struggling to get my head around all of this. I'm not sure if you're evil or just plain crazy, but this whole situation is bizarre. That's exactly what I said to Bernice. It's bizarre.'

'Her mother may never recover, really is there any point in bringing more sadness to Bernice?'

'She has the right to know that her mother is alive, to get a chance to speak to her, to find out the truth. It's obvious you don't give a thought to how Bernice has dealt with this. She's a wonderful woman. She doesn't deserve the pain you've caused her.' Nick trembled with anger. 'I'm going to find Bernice and tell her everything. If you know anything about her baby son, you tell me, NOW, or I swear that old hearse along the road will be busier than ever.'

Mrs McEwan looked over at Bernice's father. The man shook his head.

'Bernice has gone to the forest to find the perfect spot for her Granny's urn,' her father said.

'I'll go find her then.' Nick stood to leave.

'Please don't do or say anything yet.' Mrs McEwan held tightly to the sleeve of Nick's jacket.

'I think McShane may be in the forest, too,' Bernice's father added. 'I'd wait until she returns.'

'You cryptic old bastards, what the fuck is going on here!'

Nick headed for the door, only to find it had been locked tight.

Chapter 37

Grass pressed against her cheek like seaweed. Metal scraped stone as Bernice willed her eyes to open. Through a mesh of lashes she could see him, just beyond a small heap of earth. She recognised the boots and hacking cough. As he turned the soil, it looked darker and richer than before. She tried to cry out. Blood glued her tongue and she remained silent and motionless.

Silhouetted against the backdrop of the forest, he rested on the shovel handle and wiped his brow with his cap. A blue moon shimmered through the trees. Under different circumstances the image may have been captivating and a delight for an artist's brush.

Bernice had lost all sense of time, she urged herself to remain conscious. Her surroundings were tranquil, the silence broken mainly by his bronchial cough and the occasional screech of wildlife making their presence known.

She channelled the waning energies within her and called upon the Goddess Hecate to protect her. Lying still, she welcomed the cool dampness of the grass beneath her and let her dreams drift like tumbleweed through her mind.

* * *

Bernice walked through picturesque countryside. Instinctively she followed a ribbon of driveway along a tree-lined route. In the distance, an idyllic mansion with turrets and stained glass windows sat against a backdrop of hills and fir trees.

Bernice embraced the tranquillity of her surroundings, until she noticed a woman striding purposefully ahead; hands clasped behind her back, shoulders straight, the woman took even, deliberate steps. Her pale face, framed by wisps of frosted curls, was set in concentration. A small teddy bear peeped from beneath the woman's tweed coat: brown buttons for eyes, floppy paws dangled against frayed lapels.

Bernice followed the woman into the mansion. Afternoon tea was served by brisk waiters in sombre suits. Platters of crust-less sandwiches nestled in napkins sculpted like swans. A few guests looked up as the woman entered, removed her coat, lay it down and gently tucked the teddy bear snugly beneath its folds. The woman began to sing. Her voice was light and mystical. A lullaby from Bernice's childhood brushed her memory. She watched the woman glide regally between sofas, oblivious to the curious glances around her.

Guests fidgeted with embarrassment as she moved closer to them. Empty teacups were stirred, plates moved around like pawns on a chess-board. Bernice watched the woman weave her path with the grace of a ballerina. A tense silence hung in the air.

The woman turned towards Bernice, stopped singing, and in a soft voice murmured, 'Bernadette, I have always loved you.'

The woman's ice-grey eyes focussed beyond Bernice as she continued on her journey, arms outstretched.

'Bernadette, I love you,' she repeated, her voice becoming higher, more urgent as tears dampened her cheeks.

Bernice recognised her mother from the photograph in her father's wallet. The panic in her words clawed at Bernice's conscience.

* * *

Bernice opened her eyes slightly, adjusting to the sunlight filtering through the trees above. Shards of golden light showered over her as she raised a hand to her head to clear her view.

She was alone in the forest.

Tarot Cards The Fool and The Empress

The Meaning of —

The Fool
Carefree – Important decisions – New beginnings – Optimistic

The Fool is numbered 0 – the number of unlimited potential – and does not have a specific place in the sequence of the Tarot cards. The Fool can come either at the beginning of the Major Arcana or at the end. The Major Arcana is often considered as the Fool's journey through life and as such, he is ever present and therefore needs no number.

The Fool is a very powerful card in the Tarot deck, usually representing a new beginning and, consequently, an end to something in your old life. The Fool's position in any spread reveals which aspects of your life may be subject to change. The Fool indicates important decisions ahead which may not be easy to make and involve an element of risk for you. The changes should be approached with optimism and care to gain the most positive outcome.

The Fool starts his journey armed with boundless potential. He gazes upward toward the sky, about to take a leap into the world – but is he ready? He possess all the tools he needs in the unopened bag he carries – but does not know what he holds. His guardian (his pet) will protect him but push him to learn any lessons that he needs to learn.

The Empress
Abundant creativity – Fulfilment – Mother figure – Productivity

The Empress is the archetypal Earth Mother, the Anima, the Feminine Principle, Demeter, Freyja and the Goddess of Fertility: Ruled by Venus, the planet of love, creativity, fertility, art, harmony, luxury, beauty and grace.

The empress is inherently feminine – an earth mother ruled by Venus. She embodies love, creativity, luxury, beauty and harmony. She wears a crown of stars to signify her relationship with the angels and fairies. The forest which surrounds her alludes to her deep connection with mother earth and life. She draws energy from the water and peace from the trees, completely at one with the world around her.

Her creative energy will increase your chances of artistic success: This card also suggests a very strong possibility of pregnancy – not necessarily yours, but you might be seeing a new addition to your extended family or the family of a close friend in the near future! This card is a good signal for you and those around you.

Empress Tarot Story

Having decided what he will create with his tools, the Fool strides forward, impatient to make his future a full-grown reality. This is when he comes upon the Empress. Her hair like burnished copper, wearing a crown of stars, and a white gown dotted with pomegranates, she rests on her throne, surrounded by an abundance of grain and a lush garden.

Glossary

Not all of these terms are used in this trilogy of books but they may give the reader a better understanding of Wicca, also, this is not a comprehensive glossary as there are variations of terminology and spellings.

Air – one of the four magical elements.

Akasha – fifth element, spirit.

Altar – table or flat surface used during rituals to hold ritual tools, books, etc.

Amulet – a magical charged item, often worn around the neck for protection.

Animism – the spiritual belief that everything in nature, animate and inanimate, possesses a soul.

Ankh – ancient Egyptian symbol representing life and rebirth: similar to, but not the same as crux ansata.

Aquarius – the eleventh sign of the zodiac, ruling from January 21 – February 19. Air sign ruled by the planet Uranus.

Aradia (air-a-dee-a) – Italian goddess, claimed to be Queen of Witches by some Wiccans

Aries – the first sign of the zodiac, ruling from March 21 – April 20. Fire sign ruled by the planet Mars.

Asatru – Norse Reconstructionism; The pagan polytheistic religion of early Scandinavians (historical). Now also a Neo-pagan religion based on this.

Astral body – representation of person or things found on the astral plane.

Astral plane – a kind of dimension composed of energy.

Astral projection – an out-of-body experience, usually induced through trance and during sleep.

Athame – small, double-edged ritual dagger, usually black-handled: used to draw Circles and direct energy.

Aura – an energy field surrounding all living things.

Balefire – a sacred outdoor fire burned by some Wiccan at certain Sabbats.

Banish – to drive away or release a spirit or energy.

B.C.E. – Before Common Era: an alternate dating system corresponding to B.C.

Beltane – Sabbat held on May 1st: also known as May Day, May Eve, Rood Day, Roodmas, and Walpurgisnacht.

Besom – Broom used symbolically or literally for cleansing: sometimes jumped over as a symbol of the leap into married life after handfasting.

Big Blue Book – sometimes Uncle Bucky's Big Blue Book, refers to Buckland's Complete Book of Witchcraft, a commonly read beginner's book.

Binding – a spell which generally involves tying knots in cords or a similar action, aimed at restricting energy or actions.

Bolline – for traditionalist Witches, knife used to gather herbs, or to cut physical symbols like cords in ritual. Some may also use it to do practical things from scratching a name or symbol on a candle to scraping up the spilled wax afterwards.

Book of Illuminations – alternate name for what is traditionally called Book of Shadows.

Book of Light – alternate name for what is traditionally called Book of Shadows.

Book of Shadows – a collection of rituals, notes, spells, etc. as well as sometimes a journal of workings.

Burning Times – name given to Reformation and Inquisition, when the Church actively killed people for practicing "witchcraft".

Cakes and Ale – Wiccan ritual meal consumed during circle. May be nearly any combination of a liquid (not necessarily ale or even alcoholic: mead, wine, tea, or juice as well) and a small snack or piece of bread. Many Wiccans do this, although theological reasons given for it vary.

Calling the Quarters – after the circle is cast, the four elements are usually invited or invoked to be present, one in each of the cardinal directions, referred to as the Quarters. At the end of the ritual, immediately before the circle is opened, the Quarters are thanked and bid farewell.

Cancer – fourth sign of the zodiac, ruling from June 22 – July 22. Water sign ruled by the Moon.

Candlemas – Sabbat held on February 2nd; also known as Imbolg/Imbolc, Oimelc, or Candelaria.

Capricorn – tenth sign of the zodiac, ruling from December 23 – January 20. Earth sign ruled by the planet Saturn.

Casting a Circle – usually the beginning of a Wiccan ritual, where the ritual space is defined as separate from "normal" space. May be done symbolically by visualization or with a semi-literal outline or barrier (sprinkling sand or laying down flowers to outline the edge of the circle, for example). The reverse process, which ends a Wiccan ritual, is called Opening the Circle.

Cauldron – pot or kettle, generally used as goddess symbol.

C.E. – Common Era; an alternate dating system corresponding to A.D.

Censer – an incense burner.

Ceremonial magick – the art and practice of controlling spirits through force of will, requires dedication and study.

Cernunnos – Celtic god, often used for name of Wiccan Lord (not universally accepted).

Chakras – seven energy points within the body.

Chalice – cup used in ritual, may be almost any kind of drinking vessel. There may be one for each person or a communal one for the coven. May also be used as a symbol of the Element of Water.

Charge of the Goddess – well-known piece of poetry by Doreen Valiente.

Circle – magical construct used in rituals (see A Circle)

Cone of Power – When doing spellwork in a coven the combined energy raised is often visualized by members as a cone growing over the Circle. This is built up by the coven's actions and then released to serve a specific purpose, after which the coven grounds and centres again.

Consecration – act of blessing an object with positive energy.

Corn Dolly – a human or animal figure fashioned out of a sheaf of corn: used in spells and as fertility symbol.

Coven – a group of people who come together to do ritual and study.

Cowan – non-Wicca or non-Pagan (derogatory).

Craft – (The Craft) alternate name for Wicca or Witchcraft, borrowed from Masons.

Crone – one of the aspects of the Threefold Goddess.

Crone – older, wise woman.

Dawning Down the Sun – invoking the God into one's self, usually in ritual.

Deosil (day-o-sil) – clockwise direction, also known as "sunwise".

Dianic Wicca, also wicce – loose grouping of traditions and approaches that emphasize extremely feminist ideas and normally exclude men and possibly transwomen.

Divination – art of foretelling future events or revealing knowledge through the use of tools (eg. Tarot, runes, etc.)

Drawing Down the Moon (or Sun) (DDM, DDS) – a ritual where the High Priestess invokes the Goddess into her in a form of ritual embodiment or playing the role of an avatar. Also used for High Priest to invoke the God in some groups, then called Drawing Down the Sun.

Earth – one of the four magical elements.

Eclectic – usually means not adhering to any established tradition or set of practices: creating one's own path and potentially drawing on a wide range of sources, mixing and matching as one sees fit.

Eke-name – one's sacred and secret name, used only with the divine and/or with fellow worshippers.

Elements or Quarters – the four conceptual Elements of Air, Fire, Water, and Earth. Dates back to the ancient Greeks; today usually regarded as something more like qualities or properties than elements.

Enchantment – another word for spell.

Eostre – Spring Equinox Sabbat.

Esbat – a regular meeting of a Wiccan coven or circle, sometimes used to refer to Full or New Moon rituals.

Evocation – calling up spirits or other magical entities.

Feri – one of several variations on F(a)er(ie/y) – A Wiccan tradition that focuses on ecstatic experience, especially physical and artistic.

Fetch – a name for one's astral body

Fire – one of the four magical elements

Fivefold kiss – ritual kiss on feet, knees, near genitals, breasts/chest, and lips.

Garderian tradition – Wiccan tradition which traces unbroken lineage to Gerald Gardner.

Gematria – A Kabbalistic method of interpreting the Hebrew scriptures by computing the numerical value of words, based on the values of their constituent letters.

Gemini – the third sign of the zodiac ruling from May 22 – June 21. Air sign ruled by the planet Mercury.

God – male aspect deity: the Lord.

Goddess – female aspect deity: the Lady.

Goddess worship – all faiths where the female divinity is the major focus: not Wicca.

Great Rite – symbolic or actual sex act performed as part of a ritual: also known as "Sacred Marriage".

Green magic – low magic, magic focusing on the physical.

Green Man – representation of the Lord as ruler of the forest.

Grimoire – a book containing a collection of spells.

Ground/grounding – to root self in the physical world.

Hand, projective – energy emitting from right hand.

Hand, receptive – energy receiving left hand.

Handfasting – a Pagan marriage ceremony.

Henotheism – the belief in one or more gods, without denying the existence of other gods.

Herbalism – herbs are often used in Wicca. Many ingredients have folk names that would sound quite alarming to most of us but which actually just describe herbs. For instance, wild vanilla was sometimes referred to as deer's tongue, and dandelions were referred to as lion's tooth.

Hermes Trismegistus – "Thrice Great Hermes", teacher of the magical system known as Hermeticism.

High magic – ritual magic, magic focused on the spiritual realm.

High Priest/HP – male head of coven

High Priestess/HPS – female head of coven: representative of Goddess.

Horned God – generally seen by Wiccans as the male consort of the Goddess: male deity with stag horns rising from His head.

Imbolc/Imbolg – Sabbat held on February 2nd.

Incantation – a ritual recitation of a prayer or spell, usually rhymed, to produce a magical effect.

Invocation – calling upon a higher power (deities, Spirit, etc.) for support or assistance.

Kabbalah – occult theosophy of rabbinical origin: magical system including the Tree of Life and Gematria: also Cabala, Cabbala, Kabala or Qabbalah).

Kabbalist – one who practices Kabbalah.

Karma – the force generated by a person's actions: thought to determine the nature of one's next incarnation.

Lammas – Sabbat held on August 1st.

Left-hand path – use of magic for self-gain and/or evil purposes.

Leo – the fifth sign of the zodiac ruling from July 23 -August 21. Fire sign ruled by the Sun.

Libra – the seventh sign of the zodiac ruling from September 24 – October 23. Air sign ruled by the planet Venus.

Lineage – initiations, degrees – BTW and similar traditions are structured around initiations which are given as first degree, second degree, and third degree. Usually, a person who has a third degree initiation is an HP/S.

Lingam – a stylized phallic symbol of the masculine cosmic principle.

Litha – Summer Solstice Sabbat.

Low magic – green magic, magic generally focused on the physical.

Lughnasadh – Sabbat held on August 1st.

Mabon – Fall Equinox Sabbat.

Magic – "The Science and Art of causing Change to occur in conformity with Will" – A. Crowley

Magick, Majic, Majick – alternate spellings for magic (not accepted by all).

Maiden – one of the aspects of the Threefold Goddess – female assistant to High Priestess in some traditions.

Meditation – the act of engaging in quiet contemplation or reflection.

Midsummer – summer Solstice Sabbat.

Mother – one of the aspects of the Threefold Goddess.

Neo-Paganism – an umbrella term, referring to modern-day practices which aim to revive nature religions, goddess-worship and/or mystery traditions.

New Age – A broad movement characterized by alternative approaches to traditional Western culture, with an interest in spirituality, mysticism, holism, and environmentalism.

Numerology – a method of divination that analyses the symbolism of numbers.

Old Ones – name encompassing all gods and goddess.

Old Religion – used to refer to Witchcraft, Paganism, and/or Wicca (lots of differing opinions here as to its correctness).

Once-born – non-Wiccan (derogatory).

Ostara – Spring Equinox Sabbat.

Pagan – one who is not Christian, Muslim or Jewish.

Pagan – a follower of an Earth-Based religion.

Pantheism – belief in or worship of more than one god belonging to more than one pantheon.

Pentacle – five-pointed star, three dimensional, a talisman or magical object, typically disc-shaped and inscribed with a pentagram, used as a symbol of the element of earth.

Pentagram – five-pointed star, two dimensional, A five-pointed star that is formed by drawing a continuous line in five straight segments, often used as a mystic and magical symbol. Compare with pentacle

Pisces – the twelfth sign of the zodiac ruling from February 20 - March 20: Water sign ruled by the planets Jupiter and Neptune.

Polytheism – belief in or worship of more than one god.

Querent – in divination, the person who asks the questions of the reader.

Rede/Wiccan Rede – "An it harm none, do what thou will".

Ritual – a religious or magical ceremony, characterized by formalized actions and words.

Ritual magic – high magic, magic focusing on the spiritual realm.

Runes – divination tool using symbols carved into wood or stone.

Runes – symbols, early alphabet.

Sabbats – the eight holy days based on the seasons.

Sagittarius – the ninth sign of the zodiac ruling from November 23 – December 22: Fire sign ruled by the planet Jupiter.

Samhain – Sabbat held on October 31st.

Scorpio – the eighth sign of the zodiac ruling from October 24 – November 22: Water sign ruled by the planets Mars and Pluto.

Scry – gaze into or at an object with the intent to see future events or distant places.

Skyclad – Wiccan term for ritual nudity as a symbol of the trust and openness between participants. Almost always occurs in closed groups.

Solitary – a name given to Wiccans or other pagans who work and worship alone.

Spell – a magical working aimed at changing reality.

Spirit – the fifth (yes, fifth) of the four magical elements.

Spirit – an animating or vital principle within all living beings.

Spirit – a discarnate entity, such as a ghost or apparition.

Sympathetic magic – magic which works on the principle that like attracts like: image magic, creative visualization.

Talisman – object marked with magical signs, used for protection or to attract beneficial energy.

Tarot cards – set of 78 cards, 22 Major Arcana and 56 Minor Arcana: used for self-discovery or divination.

Taurus – the second sign of the zodiac ruling from April 21 – May 21: Earth sign ruled by the planet Venus.

Theism – belief in the existence of a god or gods.

Threefold Goddess – Maiden, Mother and Crone: goddess with three changing faces.

Threefold Law – belief that all actions, good or bad, are returned three times over.

Tradition – group of covens sharing a common lineage, rituals, and beliefs.

Uncle Al – refers to Aleister Crowley, who is believed to have influenced Gerald Gardner, the Father of Wicca.

Virgo – the sixth sign of the zodiac ruling from August 22 – September 23: an Earth sign ruled by the planet Mercury.

Wand – ritual tool, usually made of wood and 21" in length.

Water – one of the four magical elements

Wheel of the Year – a term used by Wiccans to mean one complete cycle of the year, encompassing all eight Sabbats.

Wicca – Earth-Based religion.

Wiccan – follower of Wicca.

Wiccaning – a Wiccan birth rite where the Lord and Lady are asked to watch over the baby.

Widdershins – counterclockwise direction.

Witch – practitioner of witchcraft.

Witchcraft – art of spell casting, focusing mainly on low magic.

Yang – in Taoism, the active, male, positive principle.

Yin – in Taoism, the passive, female, negative principle.

Yoni – a stylized representation of the female genitalia symbolizing the feminine principle.

Yule – Winter Solstice Sabbat.

A note from the author

Thank you for reading "Don't Doubt the Magic". If you have enjoyed this book please feel free to post a review on your favourite review site.
Please contact me via my website at any time.
www.cathiedevitt.com

The journey continues... Part Three in this Trilogy is due for release in 2017

Roundfire

FICTION

Put simply, we publish great stories. Whether it's literary or popular, a gentle tale or a pulsating thriller, the connecting theme in all Roundfire fiction titles is that once you pick them up you won't want to put them down.
If you have enjoyed this book, why not tell other readers by posting a review on your preferred book site. Recent bestsellers from Roundfire are:

The Bookseller's Sonnets
Andi Rosenthal

The Bookseller's Sonnets intertwines three love stories with a tale of religious identity and mystery spanning five hundred years and three countries.
Paperback: 978-1-84694-342-3 ebook: 978-184694-626-4

Birds of the Nile
An Egyptian Adventure
N.E. David

Ex-diplomat Michael Blake wanted a quiet birding trip up the Nile – he wasn't expecting a revolution.
Paperback: 978-1-78279-158-4 ebook: 978-1-78279-157-7

Blood Profit$
The Lithium Conspiracy
J. Victor Tomaszek, James N. Patrick, Sr.

The blood of the many for the profits of the few... *Blood Profit$*
will take you into the cigar-smoke-filled room where American
policy and laws are really made.
Paperback: 978-1-78279-483-7 ebook: 978-1-78279-277-2

The Burden
A Family Saga
N.E. David

Frank will do anything to keep his mother and father apart. But
he's carrying baggage – and it might just weigh him down ...
Paperback: 978-1-78279-936-8 ebook: 978-1-78279-937-5

The Cause
Roderick Vincent

The second American Revolution will be a fire lit from an
internal spark.
Paperback: 978-1-78279-763-0 ebook: 978-1-78279-762-3

Don't Drink and Fly
The Story of Bernice O'Hanlon: Part One
Cathie Devitt

Bernice is a witch living in Glasgow. She loses her way in her
life and wanders off the beaten track looking for the garden of
enlightenment.
Paperback: 978-1-78279-016-7 ebook: 978-1-78279-015-0

Gag
Melissa Unger

One rainy afternoon in a Brooklyn diner, Peter Howland punctures an egg with his fork. Repulsed, Peter pushes the plate away and never eats again.
Paperback: 978-1-78279-564-3 ebook: 978-1-78279-563-6

The Master Yeshua
The Undiscovered Gospel of Joseph
Joyce Luck

Jesus is not who you think he is. The year is 75 CE. Joseph ben Jude is frail and ailing, but he has a prophecy to fulfil …
Paperback: 978-1-78279-974-0 ebook: 978-1-78279-975-7

On the Far Side, There's a Boy
Paula Coston

Martine Haslett, a thirty-something 1980s woman, plays hard on the fringes of the London drag club scene until one night which prompts her to sign up to a charity. She writes to a young Sri Lankan boy, with consequences far and long.
Paperback: 978-1-78279-574-2 ebook: 978-1-78279-573-5

Tuareg
Alberto Vazquez-Figueroa

With over 5 million copies sold worldwide, *Tuareg* is a classic adventure story from best-selling author Alberto Vazquez-Figueroa, about honour, revenge and a clash of cultures.
Paperback: 978-1-84694-192-4

Readers of ebooks can buy or view any of these bestsellers by clicking on the live link in the title. Most titles are published in paperback and as an ebook. Paperbacks are available in traditional bookshops. Both print and ebook formats are available online.

Find more titles and sign up to our readers' newsletter at http://www.johnhuntpublishing.com/fiction

Follow us on Facebook at https://www.facebook.com/JHPfiction and Twitter at https://twitter.com/JHPFiction